Engaging the Snark

Engaging the Snark

A Textual Commentary on
The Hunting of the Snark

By

Lewis Carroll

ILLUSTRATED BY
HENRY HOLIDAY

INTRODUCTION AND ANNOTATIONS BY
SELWYN GOODACRE

evertype

2024

Published by Evertype, 19A Corso Street, Dundee, DD2 1DR, Scotland.
www.evertype.com.

Introduction and annotations © 2024 Selwyn Goodacre.
This edition © 2024 Michael Everson.

First edition July 2024.

A catalogue record for this book is available from the British Library.

ISBN-10 1-78201-311-3
ISBN-13 978-1-78201-311-2

Typeset in De Vinne Text, Mona Lisa, ENGRAVERS' ROMAN, and *Liberty* by
Michael Everson.

Illustrations: Henry Holiday, 1876.

Cover: Michael Everson.

For Alan Tannenbaum,
expert on all aspects of *The Snark*,
and a great collecto

Contents

Introduction

As I said in the introductions to my books *Elucidating Alice*[1] and *Reflecting Alice*,[2] surely we already have the *Annotated Alice*. I tried to explain why I wanted to do my own annotations. The same situation of course applies with *The Hunting of the Snark*. We already have *The Annotated Snark* so brilliantly realized by the great Martin Gardner,[3] and I bow to that important book. There you will find full backgrounds to many important features of the poem, and I myself contributed to the "definitive" edition of his work (a revision of my earlier *The Listing of the Snark*—for which the present edition has an updated version!).

1   Lewis Carroll. 2015. *Elucidating Alice: A Textual Commentary on Alice's Adventures in Wonderland*. Introduction and Annotations by Swlwyn Goodacre, illustrations by John Tenniel. Evertype. ISBN 978-1-78201-105-7.

2   Lewis Carroll. 2015. *Reflecting Alice: A Textual Commentary on Through the Looking-Glass*. Introduction and Annotations by Swlwyn Goodacre, illustrations by John Tenniel. Evertype. ISBN 978-1-78201-223-8.

3   Lewis Carroll. 2006. *The Annotated Hunting of the Snark: The Definitive Edition*. Edited with notes by Martin Gardner, illustrations by Henry Holiday and others, introduction by Adam Gopnik. W. W. Norton. ISBN 978-0-393-06242-7.

But as with my work on the *Alice* books I want to concentrate on the actual text—to look how the poem is structured, and comment on the poetic elements. My sister Margaret wrote a most perceptive article,[4] and I have included a number of her insights into my annotations. She views the poem as a type of ballad, which she says "must be a narrative; tell a story of immediate and gripping interest, of the mysteries of life and death, of love, and hate". She says "the traditional journey is seen in Dante, Homer and Chaucer (e.g. in the dramatic tale of 'The Wife of Usher's Well')".

Carroll chooses a fast-running rhythm throughout the eight Fits—a feature Snark Clubs appreciate as the saga reads aloud so very well.

The story of the genesis of this great poem is fascinating.

Lewis Carroll had published *Alice's Adventures in Wonderland* in 1865, and its sequel *Through the Looking-Glass* in 1871. By then both books were assured best sellers, yet he made a clear decision to write no further sequels. He himself later recorded that, with *Alice* he was making "a desperate attempt to strike out some new line of fairy-lore". The urge for originality was strong, but the *Alice* vein had run its course.

Lewis Carroll insisted that with all his inspirational work "every new-born idea 'comes of itself'". He did not wait long for the arrival of new inspiration.

After a busy Spring in 1874, Dodgson spent the latter half of June on holiday at Sandown on the Isle of Wight. On 30 June, he went to stay at the family home at Guildford, only to find that his cousin and godson, Charles Wilcox, was ill with tuberculosis.

---

4   Margaret Goodacre. 1985. "The Hunting of the Snark—a Study", in *Jabberwocky, the Journal of the Lewis Carroll Society*. Spring.

He made a brief visit to Oxford, but returned to Guildford on 17 July in order to take his part in the nursing of his cousin. He stayed up most of that first night with him. The next day, after only three hours sleep, he went for a walk on the Downs. Let Lewis Carroll take up the story:

> I was walking on a hillside, alone, one bright summer day, when suddenly there came into my head one line of verse—one solitary line—"For the Snark *was* a Boojum, you see." I knew not what it meant, then: I know not what it means, now; but I wrote it down: and, sometime afterwards, the rest of the stanza occurred to me, that being its last line: and so by degrees, at odd moments during the next year or two, the rest of the poem pieced itself together, that being its last stanza.

Morton Cohen[5] has suggested that the walk, acting, as it were, as "an escape into a brighter and healthier world", allowed deep personal defences to come to the rescue of his troubled spirits as his sensitive and artistic temperament enjoyed a "brief respite from the bleak realities at the family home". As his mind relaxed, the nonsense line entered unbidden.

At first, Carroll intended the poem to be part of a projected children's book (presumably *Sylvie and Bruno*, eventually published in 1889). By the early Autumn of 1874, it consisted of three Fits ("The Landing", "The Hunting", "The Vanishing"), with possibly the whole, or parts of "The Bellman's Speech" and "The Baker's Tale".

At about this time, he approached the artist Henry Holiday to illustrate the poem. Although not a true Pre-Raphaelite,

---

5   Morton Cohen. 1976. "Hark the Snark", in *Lewis Carroll Observed*. Edited by Edward Guiliano. New York: Clarkson N. Potter.

Holiday belonged to a group of artists associated with the later elements of that movement. Apart from *The Hunting of the Snark* he is chiefly remembered today as a designer of stained glass windows. Carroll had known him for some years and had occasionally used his home as a photography studio.

Holiday records that initially three pictures were commissioned, and soon after, a fourth. By November, one ("The Landing") was cut on wood. But Carroll was suddenly afflicted with doubts. He consulted Ruskin, who was less than enthusiastic, "holding out no hopes that Holiday would be able to illustrate the book satisfactorily". The reasons for this lack of enthusiasm are not recorded. But it was enough to cause the entire project to lay in abeyance.

Further stimulus was necessary. Typically it came in the form of a new friendship with a child—the eight-year-old Gertrude Chataway, whom he met on the beach at Sandown in September 1875. He decided to publish the poem as a Christmas book, and dedicate it to Gertrude. He even composed the dedicatory poem—well before completion of the poem itself.

More and more stanzas were written that Autumn, and Henry Holiday has recorded how further pictures were requested. By November there were 88 stanzas, and six pictures. Lewis Carroll thought the poem was finished. From Journal entries it is possible to assess what this "complete" poem (of five Fits) consisted of Fits I–IV ("The Landing", "The Bellman's Speech", "The Baker's Tale", "The Hunting"), which we we know were complete. Fit V at the time would have consisted of the "refrain" stanza ("They sought it with thimbles...") plus stanzas 2, 3, 5, and 6 of Fit VII (as we now know it), with the present Fit VIII running straight on from it.

During November 1875, Carroll wrote two more Fits—the ones we now know as Fits V and VI ("The Beaver's Lesson" and "The Barrister's Dream"). The two new pictures for these were drawn. The "old" Fit V was rearranged to make two Fits. Five stanzas were added to the ones noted above, to fill out the story of "The Banker's Fate"; this became Fit VII. The refrain stanza was moved to start Fit VIII ("The Vanishing") which now dealt purely with the climax, giving the poem a much improved dramatic conclusion.

The 141 stanzas were written and the poem was complete.

It is also possible to chart the development of Holiday's pictures, helped by reference to three groups of preliminary drawings—one in a private American collection, another in the Parrish collection at Princeton University Library, and the third at the Bryn Mawr College Library.

The first picture to be completed (Autumn 1874) was almost certainly of the Snark as Boojum. Carroll rejected it, preferring the Boojum to remain unimaginable. On the verso of a sketch for the replacement picture of "The Vanishing", there are life studies for "The Crew on Board" and "The Hunting", which certainly suggest these were the three referred to by Holiday. The latter two are of crucial importance to the poem as a whole—one portrays the crew on board, the other the all important refrain stanza. It is logical to deduce that these were the first to be drawn. Indeed, these three pictures alone would be sufficient to illustrate the three Fits that made up that first provisional text.

In fact, Holiday records that he was working on a fourth picture while still working on the first three. Also on the sheet with the life studies mentioned above, are studies for parts of "The Baker's Tale", which identifies this as the most likely candidate.

Along one side of this sheet of studies, is a list of six subjects, written in pencil by Holiday. It appears to be in chronological order, but of commission rather than when executed—the first four are those I have listed above. Holiday then lists "Bellman" (the picture that was to become the frontispiece, but which we shall refer to as "The Landing") and "Butcher" (the third picture for Fit I—showing the Butcher and Beaver on deck). The drawings for the first four pictures are in ink—as is the existing drawing for "The Butcher and Beaver". "The Landing", like the drawings for the last three pictures, is in pencil.

In a journal entry for 13 November 1875, Dodgson anticipated a total of seven pictures. Charles Mitchell[6] has suggested that the seventh would be the one for "The Barrister's Dream", since one of the Princeton sheets has life studies for "The Beaver's Lesson" and "The Banker's Fate" on the same page, suggesting they were executed at about the same time, i.e. they were the last two to be drawn (we noted above that "The Banker's Fate" was most likely to have been the last Fit to be completed).

Finished drawings survive for all the nine illustrations. All but three are about the same size as the woodblocks. It is significant that the ones that are larger are the three highly-detailed pictures—"The Crew on Board", "The Hunting", and "The Beaver's Lesson". Holiday (in his *Reminiscences of My Life*) has recorded that he treated his line drawings with "a strict view to the process" to which they would be subjected in wood engraving. This would account for the astonishing similarity between these finished drawings and the printed result.

The Snark was Holiday's first venture into book illustration. He followed the accepted procedure at that time of first producing a finished drawing, then tracing the

6   "The Design for the Snark", by Charles Mitchell, in Lewis Carroll's *The Hunting of the Snark*, Illustrated by Henry Holiday—Centennial Edition. Edited by James Tanis and John Dooley. Los Altos: William Kaufmann, Inc. in cooperation with Bryn Mawr College Library, 1981.

outlines in reverse on to the woodblock, before finishing the design again on the block, for engraver, Joseph Swain, to reproduce. Mitchell[4] notes that at the start of the project Holiday completed the finished drawings in ink, in order to gain an idea of what they would look like after engraving. As he became more proficient, he simply completed the initial drawings in pencil.

Holiday's skill as a designer of stained glass windows can be seen in some of the *Snark* pictures—particularly "The Crew on Board" which is divided in sections almost as if by the lead of the window. In "The Hunting", the lines of the anchor held by "Hope" and the array of forks give the same feel. The figures of "Hope" and "Care" have many similarities with his personifications of virtue which are often found in windows he designed (examples can be seen in Tamworth Parish Church in Staffordshire, for instance).

As with Tenniel and the *Alice* books, the characters are portrayed with heads which are too large for the bodies. In *Alice* this may have been partly in order to bring them down to Alice's size. In the *Snark*, the element of caricature is important. Curiously, the Bellman is occasionally correctly proportioned (in "The Landing"), but is in "big-head" mode on the front cover, and in "The Crew on Board".

There are other inconsistencies in Holiday's characterizations. The Banker in "The Crew on Board" looks quite different from his appearance in "The Landing", hair appears on the front of the scalp, where previously he is quite bald, and by the time we reach "The Banker's Fate" he has a veritable mop. The Butcher in the "Butcher and Beaver" looks just like a school boy. He is growing up rapidly by the time he is involved with "The Beaver's Lesson" and "The Banker's Fate".

These anomalies may be explained by the interval in time between the creation of the various pictures, the inconsistencies certainly bridge the known gaps. Even so it is curious—one would like to think it was Holiday's own contribution to the nonsense of the poem, but this does not seem very likely.

And what of the poem itself? Lewis Carroll explained it all several times (all discussed by Martin Gardner). Lewis Carroll conclusively summarising the position in 1896: "I'm very much afraid I didn't mean anything but nonsense."

Nonsense yes—the grand assumption of the truth of a totally implausible situation, supported by accurately observed detail that within its narrow confines is totally plausible. The Butcher explains a totally absurd mathematical sum, but the Beaver responds with a wonderfully observed confession, which in any *other* context would be totally suitable:

> While the Beaver confessed, with affectionate looks
> More eloquent even than tears,
> It had learned in ten minutes far more than all books
> Would have taught it in seventy years.

This is humour—and nonsense—of the highest order. No wonder that *The Hunting of the Snark* has been universally acknowledged as the greatest of all epic nonsense poems. Indeed, what rivals are there?

Acknowledgements

I am a member of more than one "Snark Club", at which I have given the occasional talk. Much of this book has grown out of some of those talks, and I am most grateful to their members for their ongoing support and encouragement.

A NOTE ON THE TEXT

Lewis Carroll made a number of small changes when the poem was reprinted as part of *Rhyme? and Reason?* (Macmillan 1883). I listed the changes in *Jabberwocky, the Journal of the Lewis Carroll Society* Autumn 1976, and these changes have been incorporated in this edition. They include changes in the dedication poem and in the Preface.

Concerning the Poetic Structure of the Poem

*M*uch of what follows is thanks to the study by Margaret Goodacre (see reference above). The traditional ballad metre has a 4-line stanza with a particular rhyme pattern: *abab* or *abcb* on the end word of each line (quatrain). In this poem Carroll uses mostly *abab*, but occasionally *abcb* (Instances are uncommon and they will be noted in the text with ❸). Our Author also occasionally has an internal rhyme in line 1 (these will be noted by ①) and occasionally an internal rhyme in line 3 ((noted by ③)

Technically a line of verse is divided into a number of feet—each foot is a group of beats (or syllables), in 2-time (duple rhythm), or 3-time (triple rhythm). In duple rhythm there are four patterns, but only one need concern us here—the "iamb", which is "short, long", notationally represented as ˘ ´ ˘. In triple rhythm there are three patterns:

Anapaestic—"short, short, long":   ˘ ˘ ´
Amphibraic—"short, long, short":   ˘ ´ ˘
Dactylic—"long, long, short":   ´ ´ ˘

Carroll uses a fast, running rhythm throughout the eight Fits, chiefly anapaests and amphibrachs. The famous repeated verse provides an example:

> Thĕy soúght ĭt | wĭth thímblĕs, | thĕy sóught ĭt | wĭth cáre;
> Thĕy pŭrsúed | ĭt wĭth fórks | aňd hópe;
> Thĕy thréatĕned | ĭts lífe wĭth ă | ráilwăy | -shăre;
> Thĕy chármed ĭt | wĭth smíles aňd | sóap.

This is a curious and comic use of triple rhythm, the length of each line being different, but the key words are stressed carefully and rhythmically, according to the sense or nonsense. A particularly good examples of a fast triple rhythm reflects here the nervous excitement and the fast beating heart of the Beaver in Fit V when:

> Thĕ Béavĕr | tŭrned pále tŏ | thĕ típ ŏf | ĭts táil

(Three amphibrachs, one iamb) and later in Fit VII:

> Wĕnt bóundĭng | ălóng ŏn | thĕ típ ŏf | ĭts táil,

Regular anapaesic lines occur especially in straight description:

> Thĕre wăs óne | whŏ wăs fámed | fŏr thĕ núm | bĕr ŏf thíngs

Four anapaests; and even when exclamations are included the triple rhythm is dominant

> Hĕ wŏuld áns | wĕr tŏ "Hí!" | ŏr tŏ án | ў lŏud crý,
>   Sŭch ăs "Frý | mĕ!" ŏr "Frít | tĕr mў wĭg!"
> Tŏ "Whát | -yŏu-măy-cáll- | ŭm!" ŏr "Whát | -wăs-hĭs-náme!"
>   Bŭt ĕspéci | ăllў "Thíng- | ŭm-ă-jíg!"

The Snark from 1876

*T*he early publishing history of the book is complicated and full of interest. The basic facts I set out in my early book *The Listing of the Snark* (privately printed in 1974, and updated in the sources given in the four footnotes above). Apart from the regular buff binding of the first edition, a number of copies were bound in blue, green, red, or white vellum—mostly issued for presentation. Some copies of the first edition are known with a printed dust jacket—a very early example of such items; surviving examples are rare The book reached the 18th thousand by the end of 1876. In 1884 it became part of *Rhyme? and Reason?* But in 1890 it was again issued on its own, and remained in print in this form until 1920. Macmillan issued a "miniature edition" in 1910, frequently reprinted, before going out of print in 1948.

In the USA James Osgood of Boston issued a miniature pirated edition in 1876, with a reprint the same year. Macmillan in New York issued a regular edition in 1890, frequently reprinted, before going out of print in 1937. Several other publishers also issued their versions in the USA from 1896 onwards, including three by the Peter Pauper Press (1932, 1939 and 1952). In the UK Mervyn

Peake memorably illustrated the book in 1941—this went on to be reprinted frequently. Other important illustrators in the 1950s to 1970s issued their interpretations—Harold Jones, Helen Oxenbury, Ralph Steadman, John Minnion, Barry Moser, Byron Sewell (more than once!), Quentin Blake, and John Vernon Lord, some of these were stimulated by the 1976 centenary.

As I mentioned above. the poem reads aloud very well—and Snark Clubs began to appear as early as 1879—the idea being of course that the poem could be read out loud by the members during the course of an elaborate dinner. I acquired a Snark club menu dated 1882—with the most elaborate eight course dinner (one for each Fit). Sadly the story of these early clubs is lost in mystery. A prestigious club (the Cambridge Snark Club) was founded in 1934, and still meets annually to this day , and I am proud to be a member of it. Martin Gardner gives an amusing account of the Club in the introduction to the Penguin edition of *The Annotated Snark.*

A major landmark of course was the publishing of Martin Gardner's *The Annotated Snark* in 1962 (Simon and Schuster, New York) This brilliant book was revised, and reprinted by Penguin Books, in the UK in 1967. This was hugely successful and went through many reprints. It was further revised for the Kaufmann Centennial Edition of *The Hunting of the Snark* in 1981, which also included a revised version of my *The Listing of the Snark* .(the price for the Kaufmann Subscriber's Edition limited to 395 numbered copies was several hundred pounds—a bit of rise from the one shilling for my book though the Kaufmann edition did of course contain a lot more than my humble contribution). In 2006 my book *All the Snarks, The Illustrated Editions of The Hunting of the Snark, An Illustrated Exploration and Check List*: was published by the Inky Parrot Press, Oxford.

In 1974, members of the Newcastle Snark Club held an extra meeting met in Guildford, and re-enacted the famous walk by Lewis Carroll in 1874 when the last line of the poem came into his head (see above). A small section of the event was filmed by the BBC—we believe the film still exists. I issued my privately printed *Listing of the Snark* to celebrate the occasion. I had a patient who owned a typewriter that used a small type-face. She kindly typed the text out for me, which I had photo-copied and we had covers printed by a small local one-room printing press (the Regent Press, Church Gresley). I sold copies at 1/– each. Martin Gardner asked me to update it and it duly appeared in the book referenced above in note 4.

There has been something of an explosion of interest in the poem in the last 40 years or so. Sequels and extra verses have been created, many diverse and extraordinary opinions have been expressed as to the deeper meanings of the poem. Most of them to my mind far too academic and abstruse to be taken too seriously—in spite of their special pleading.

In 2021, Dayna Nuhn Lozinski, along with her husband Michael, and Carroll scholars Mark and Catherine Richards established the "Institute of Snarkology" and issued *The Snarkologist*, Vol.1, Fit 1, in May of that year. They have now issued a further six "Fits". The periodical publishes fine scholarly articles on all aspects relating to *The Snark*.

Fuller details of all editions over the years can be found in the expanded version of my original "Listing of the Snark" (mentioned several times above!) which is included in this book, following the text of the poem.

The Hunting
of the Snark

INSCRIBED TO A DEAR CHILD:
IN MEMORY OF GOLDEN SUMMER HOURS
AND WHISPERS OF A SUMMER SEA

Girt with a boyish garb for a boyish task,
* Eager she wields her spade: yet loves as well*
Rest on a friendly knee, intent to ask
* The tale one loves[7] to tell.*

Rude scoffer[8] of the seething outer strife,
* Unmeet to read her pure and simple spright*
Deem, if thou wilt,[9] such hours a waste of life,
* Empty of all delight!*

Chat on, sweet Maid, and rescue from annoy
* Hearts that by wiser talk are unbeguiled*
Ah, happy he who owns that tenderest joy,
* The heart-love of a child!*

---

7   In the first edition, 'one loves' read 'he loves'.

8   In the first edition, 'Rude scoffer' read 'Rude Spirit'.

9   In the first edition, 'if thou wilt' read 'if you list'.

Away, fond thoughts, and vex my soul no more!
Work claims my wakeful nights, my busy days
Albeit bright memories of that sunlit shore
Yet haunt my dreaming gaze![10]

---

10   It should of course be added that this is a double acrostic poem, the initial
letters spell out the name of the dedicatee Getrude Chataway, and her
name is divided into the initial words of each verse.

Preface

If——and the thing is wildly possible——the charge of writing nonsense were ever brought against the author of this brief but instructive poem, it would be based, I feel convinced, on the line (in p. 26)

> "Then the bowsprit got mixed with the rudder sometimes."

In view of this painful possibility, I will not (as I might) appeal indignantly to my other writings that I am incapable of such a deed: I will not (as I might) point out the strong moral purpose of this poem itself, to the arithmetical principles so cautiously inculcated in it, or to its noble teaching in Natural History——I will take the more prosaic course of simply explaining how it happened.

The Bellman, who was almost morbidly sensitive about appearances, used to have the bowsprit unshipped once or twice a week to be revarnished; and it more than once happened, when the time came for replacing it, that no one on board could remember which end of the ship it belonged to. They knew it was not of the slightest use to appeal to the

Bellman about it——he would only refer to his Naval Code, and read out in pathetic tones Admiralty Instructions which none of them had ever been able to understand——so it generally end up appearances, used being fastened on, anyhow, across the rudder. The helmsman* used to stand: by with tears in his eyes: *he* knew it was all wrong, but alas! Rule 42 of the Code. *"No one shall speak to the Man at the Helm,"* had been completed by the Bellman himself with the words *"and the Man at the Helm shall speak to no one."* So remonstrance was impossible, and no steering could be done till the next varnishing day. During these bewildering intervals the ship usually sailed backwards.

As this poem is to some extent connected with the lay of the Jabberwock, let me take this opportunity of answering a question that has often been asked me, how to pronounce "slithy toves". The "i" in "slithy" is long, as in "writhe"; and "toves" is pronounced so as to rhyme with "groves". Again the first "o" in "borogoves" is pronounced like the "o" in "borrow". I have heard people trying to give it the sound of the "o" in "worry". Such is Human Perversity.

This also seems a fitting occasion[11] to notice the other hard words in that poem. Humpty Dumpty's theory of two meanings packed into one word like a portmanteau, seems to me the right explanation for all.[12]

---

*   This office was usually undertaken by the Boots, who found in it a refuge from the Baker's constant complaints about the insufficient blacking of his three pair of boots.

11   *fitting occasion*—possibly a reference to the poem being in fits?

12   Carroll's observations on the hard words are surely not as complete as he seems to suggest. Some words are indeed most likely portmanteau— *whiffling* (whistle and sniff or sniffle?), *tulgey* (turgid and ugly?), *burbled* (bubble and gurgle?), *galumphing* (gallop and triumph?), *chortled* (chuckle and snort?)). But Carroll never gave us explanations for *vorpal, frabjous, manxome, Tumtum, Callooh, Callay,* nor indeed the *Jubjub bird* and *Bandersnatch,* both of which feature in this poem.

For instance, take the two words "fuming" and "furious". Make your mind up that you will say both words, but leave it unsettled which you will say first. Now open your mouth and speak. If your thoughts incline ever so little towards "fuming" you will say "fuming-furious"; if they turn by even a hair's breadth, towards "furious" you will say "furious-fuming"; but if you have that rarest of gifts, a perfectly balanced mind, you will say "frumious".

Supposing that, when Pistol uttered the well-known words—[13]

"Under which king, Bezonian? Speak or die!"

Justice Shallow had felt certain that it was either William or Richard, but had not been able to settle which, so that he could not possibly say either name before the other, can it be doubted that, rather than die, he would have gasped out "Rilchiam!"

Lewis Carroll

---

[13] Our Author may well say that Pistol's words are "well-known words", but they are certainly not well known to me. The quotation is from Act V Scene III of Shakespeare's play Henry IV Part 2, which reads:

PISTOL: Under which king, Bezonian? Speak, or die.

SHALLOW: Under King Harry

PISTOL: Harry the Fourth—or Fifth?

SHALLOW: Harry the Fourth

So Shallow would have been wrong with either Richard or William. A delightful hidden joke by our Author. (For your interest, Bezonian is an archaic word meaning either a "military recruit" or "a mean dishonest person or scoundrel".)

Contents

Fit I
The Landing

The Landing

"Just the place for a Snark!" the Bellman cried,[14]
　　As he landed his crew with care;
Supporting each man on the top of the tide[15]
　　By a finger entwined in his hair.

"Just the place for a Snark! I have said it twice:
　　That alone should encourage the crew.
Just the place for a Snark! I have said it thrice:
　　What I tell you three times is true."[16]

14　How does he know it is a good place for hunting a Snark?. We are given no reason, though obviously the Bellman does have them as he professes to know about Snarks, as we hear later in the saga with his detailed descriptions. So, presumably he is, no doubt, knowledgeable about possible locations for a profitable hunt.

15　And if he is able to support each man as described he would appear to be not only very strong but also rather bigger than other members of the crew. But this is no doubt our author enjoying some exaggeration for dramatic effect.

16　The last line is the first time this dictum has been stated—now part of the language.

The crew was complete: it included a Boots—
  A maker of Bonnets and Hoods—
A Barrister, brought to arrange their disputes—
  And a Broker, to value their goods.[17]

A Billiard-marker, whose skill was immense,
  Might perhaps have won more than his share—[18]
But a Banker, engaged at enormous expense,
  Had the whole of their cash in his care.

There was also a Beaver, that paced on the deck,
  Or would sit making lace in the bow:
And had often (the Bellman said) saved them from
  wreck,
  Though none of the sailors knew how.

---

17 We immediately understand that all the crew's named occupations begin
    with a B. It is interesting that we are never told the actual names of any
    members of the crew.

18 *more than his share*—from what?

There was one who was famed for the number of things
 He forgot when he entered the ship:
His umbrella, his watch, all his jewels and rings,
 And the clothes he had bought for the trip.[19]

He had forty-two boxes, all carefully packed,
 With his name painted clearly on each:[20]
But, since he omitted to mention the fact,
 They were all left behind on the beach.

The loss of his clothes hardly mattered, because
 He had seven coats on when he came,
With three pair of boots[21]—but the worst of it was,
 He had wholly forgotten his name.

---

19 *bought for the trip*—one wonders of "brought" might fit the concept more clearly.

20 *name painted clearly*—we assume that this refers to his given name (which we are never told -as with all the members of the crew, as I mentioned above) though we are told of several nick names (see below).

  And even though he omitted to mention it to the other crew members, one would have thought 42 boxes with his name painted clearly would stand out as obviously intended for the trip.

  At one Snark Club, of which I am a member, another member created 42 boxes with the words HIS NAME painted clearly on each.

21 *three pairs of boots*—the context suggests he was wearing these all at the same time, which seems a little difficult.

He would answer to "Hi!" or to any loud cry,
  Such as "Fry me!" or "Fritter my wig!"
To "What-you-may-call-um!" or "What-was-his-name!"
  But especially "Thing-um-a-jig!"[22]   ⑬

While, for those who preferred a more forcible word,
  He had different names from these:
His intimate friends called him "Candle-ends,"
  And his enemies "Toasted-cheese."[23]   ⑬

"His form is ungainly[24]—his intellect small—"
  (So the Bellman would often remark)—
"But his courage is perfect! And that, after all,
  Is the thing that one needs with a Snark."

---

22 This is the first verse that does not have a rhyme at the end of lines 1 and
    3. Instances are uncommon and they will be noted with ⑬.

23 We are given no reason why his friends and enemies used these epithets,
    though Martin Gardner, in his *Annotated Snark*, makes some fine
    suggestions.

24 *His form is ungainly*—we are not told till much later in the saga, that the
    Baker is "stupid and stout", which could possibly explain his "form".

He would joke with hyænas, returning their stare
    With an impudent wag of the head:[25]
And he once went a walk, paw-in-paw, with a bear,
    "Just to keep up its spirits," he said.

He came as a Baker: but owned, when too late—
    And it drove the poor Bellman half-mad—
He could only bake Bride-cake[26]—for which, I may
    state,
    No materials were to be had.

The last of the crew needs especial remark,
    Though he looked an incredible dunce:[27]
He had just one idea—but, that one being "Snark,"
    The good Bellman engaged him at once.

---

25   *wag of his head*—a feature of the Baker, we hear about it more than once, and particularly in the last Fit.

26   'Bride-cake' is an unusual name for a wedding cake. Perhaps used here as it also begins with a B.

27   *an incredible dunce*—we are not told till much later that "Dunce" was one of *his* nicknames.

He came as a Butcher: but gravely declared,
    When the ship had been sailing a week,
He could only kill Beavers.[28] The Bellman looked
    scared,
    And was almost too frightened to speak:

But at length he explained, in a tremulous tone,
    There was only one Beaver on board;
And that was a tame one he had of his own,
    Whose death would be deeply deplored.

The Beaver, who happened to hear the remark,
    Protested, with tears in its eyes,
That not even the rapture of hunting the Snark
    Could atone for that dismal surprise![29]

---

28   One would have thought that Beavers were not a usual source of meat for
most butchers. And it is slightly odd that it took him a week to make his
grave announcement, with the Beaver already present for some while.

29   Any atoning would of course be useless if he was already dead.

It strongly advised that the Butcher should be
    Conveyed in a separate ship:
But the Bellman declared that would never agree
    With the plans he had made for the trip:

Navigation was always a difficult art,
    Though with only one ship and one bell:
And he feared he must really decline, for his part,
    Undertaking another as well.[30]

The Beaver's best course was, no doubt, to procure
    A second-hand dagger-proof coat—[31]
So the Baker advised it—and next, to insure
    Its life in some Office of note:

---

30   The Bellman seems to be suggesting that navigating two ships at the same
      time was a regular practice—which seems doubtful.

31   You might suggest that a new dagger proof coat would be even better.

This the Banker[32] suggested, and offered for hire
    (On moderate terms), or for sale,
Two excellent Policies, one Against Fire,
    And one Against Damage From Hail.[33]

Yet still, ever after that sorrowful day,
    Whenever the Butcher was by,
The Beaver kept looking the opposite way,
    And appeared unaccountably shy.[34]

---

32   Some book dealers have thought that "Banker" was misprinted as "Baker" in the first edition, but in fact it was correct there. The misprint actually arose in the Miniature edition of 1911, and remained there through every reprint of that edition. In the Miniature edition the same misprint also appeared in Fit 4, verse 11. But that one was corrected—see below.

33   Useless policies of course for the situation at hand.

34   Why "unaccountably"? Surely it was highly accountable?

Fit II
The Bellman's Speech

The Bellman's Speech

The Bellman himself they all praised to the skies—
    Such a carriage, such ease and such grace![35]
Such solemnity, too! One could see he was wise,
    The moment one looked in his face!

He had bought a large map representing the sea,
    Without the least vestige of land:
And the crew were much pleased when they found it to
      be
    A map they could all understand.[36]

---

35   *Such a carriage*—the "a" is superfluous and in fact rather spoils the
     cadence of the line.

36   They could well *understand* it if blank, but it would be of rather less use as
     a map.

"What's the good of Mercator's North Poles and
    Equators,
Tropics, Zones, and Meridian Lines?"
So the Bellman would cry: and the crew would reply
    "They are merely conventional signs![37]   ①③🅑

"Other maps are such shapes, with their islands and
    capes!
But we've got our brave Captain to thank"
(So the crew would protest) "that he's bought *us* the
    best—
A perfect and absolute blank!"[38]   ①③🅑

This was charming, no doubt: but they shortly found
    out
That the Captain they trusted so well
Had only one notion for crossing the ocean,
    And that was to tingle his bell.   ①③🅑

---

37   This is the first verse in the saga to have an internal rhyme in the third line ("cry" / "reply"). It was to become a regular, though not exclusive, feature in the rest of the saga. We will mark each verse where this is present, with an ③. It is also the first verse to have an internal rhyme in line 1 again this is a regular feature though not exclusive. Where present—these will be noted by ①.

38   Blank certainly, and indeed one they could all understand, as I mentioned before.

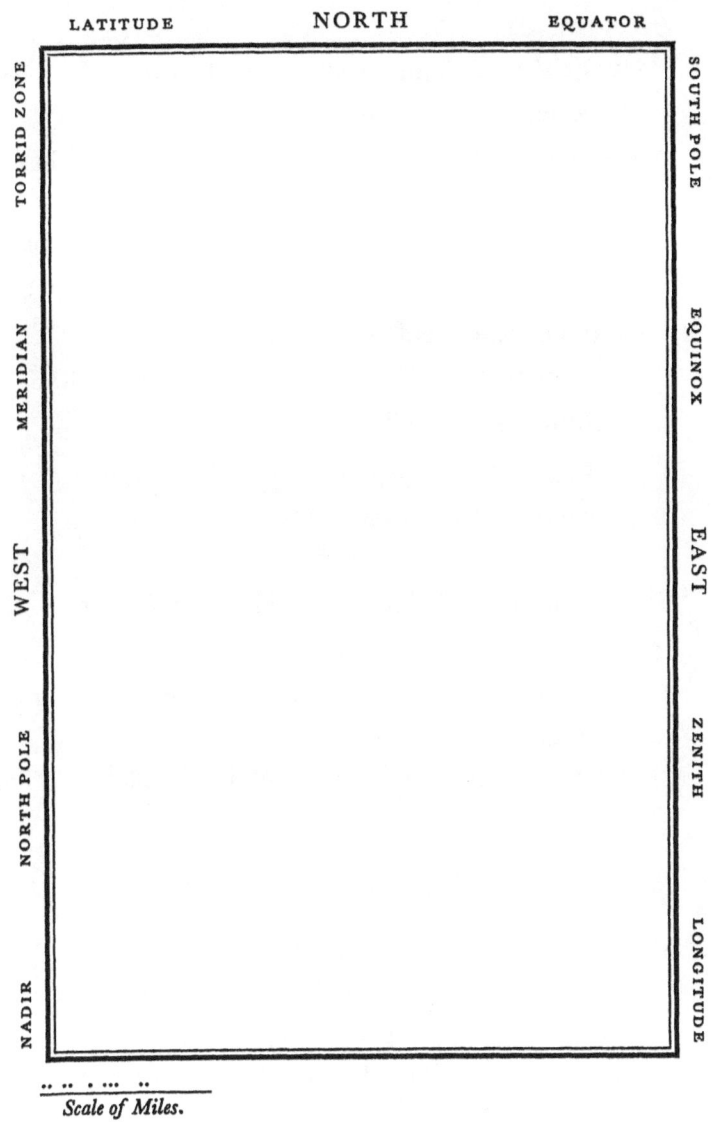

OCEAN CHART

He was thoughtful and grave—but the orders he gave
  Were enough to bewilder a crew.
When he cried "Steer to starboard, but keep her head
    larboard!"
  What on earth was the helmsman to do? ①③❸

Then the bowsprit got mixed with the rudder
    sometimes:
  A thing, as the Bellman remarked,
That frequently happens in tropical climes,
  When a vessel is, so to speak, "snarked."[39]

But the principal failing occurred in the sailing,
  And the Bellman, perplexed and distressed,
Said he *had* hoped, at least, when the wind blew due
    East,
  That the ship would *not* travel due West![40] ①③❸

---

39 The Bellman's assertion would seem to suggest that he has indeed been
    involved in previous huntings. The full explanation for this "mixing" is
    given in Carroll's Preface.

40 Carroll is possibly a little confused here. He is trying to suggest an
    impossibility (in tune with much of the saga!)—but of course a wind
    blowing "due East" blows straight towards the East, in an Easterly
    direction, and anything in its wake would indeed be pushed (and so travel)
    Eastwards.

But the danger was past—they had landed at last,
  With their boxes, portmanteaus, and bags:
Yet at first sight the crew were not pleased with the
    view
  Which consisted to chasms and crags.[41]   ①③⑬

The Bellman perceived that their spirits were low,
  And repeated in musical tone
Some jokes he had kept for a season of woe—
  But the crew would do nothing but groan.

He served out some grog with a liberal hand,
  And bade them sit down on the beach:
And they could not but own that their Captain looked
    grand,
  As he stood and delivered his speech.

---

41 The alliterating /k/ repeated here sounds sharp and cross, and the
    neighbouring /s/ and /z/ sounds hiss alongside—all demonstrate that the
    crew are disappointed with the view, but not as a possible hunting ground
    for a Snark—which seems ideal.

"Friends, Romans, and countrymen, lend me your
    ears!"
    (They were all of them fond of quotations:[42]
So they drank to his health, and they gave him three
    cheers,
    While he served out additional rations).[43]

"We have sailed many months, we have sailed many
    weeks,[44]
    (Four weeks to the month you may mark),
But never as yet ('tis your Captain who speaks)
    Have we caught the least glimpse of a Snark!

"We have sailed many weeks, we have sailed many days,
    (Seven days to the week I allow),
But a Snark, on the which we might lovingly gaze,
    We have never beheld till now!

---

42   They may well have been fond of quotations, but in fact this is wrong. The
      original quote (from Shakespeare's *Julius Caesar*) reads "Friends,
      Romans, countrymen, lend me your ears".

43   'rations' does not really rhyme with "quotations". Michael Everson notes:
      In North American English both /ˈræʃənz/ and /ˈreɪʃənz/ occur.

44   *sailed many weeks*—seems excessive, in view of the quest in hand.

"Come, listen, my men, while I tell you again[45]
    The five unmistakable marks[46]
By which you may know, wheresoever you go,
    The warranted genuine Snarks.[47]   ③ ⑬

"Let us take them in order. The first is the taste,[48]
    Which is meagre and hollow, but crisp:[49]
Like a coat that is rather too tight in the waist,
    With a flavour of Will-o-the-wisp.

"Its habit of getting up late you'll agree
    That it carries too far, when I say
That it frequently breakfasts at five o'clock tea,[50]
    And dines on the following day.[51]

---

45   You could suggest that there is an internal rhyme in line 1, but it is arguable whether "men" actually rhymes with "again".

46   The numbers of the "five marks" are all related poetically to the number of the mark in question.

47   By commenting on "warranted genuine Snarks" he appears to be suggesting that there are several fake (?) varieties of Snarks.

48   *first is the taste*—the first of the five marks. Nicely chosen by our author— using two similar sounding words—first and taste.

49   We assume that the Bellman is referring to consuming cooked portions from a Snark. In view of the following human characteristics of Snarks (discussed next), this would appear a rather dark mark, almost cannibalistic.

50   The use of "five o'clock tea" suggests a change in Victorian habits from the six o'clock tea at the Mad Tea-Party in *Alice's Adventures in Wonderland*.

51   This is the second mark, although not stated directly as such by the Bellman. Our author is using "second"; in two different senses—one as a number, and one indicating the use of time.

"The third is its slowness in taking a jest.[52]
Should you happen to venture on one,
It will sigh like a thing that is deeply distressed:
And it always looks grave at a pun.

"The fourth is its fondness[53] for bathing-machines,[54]
Which it constantly carries about,
And believes that they add to the beauty of scenes—
A sentiment open to doubt.

"The fifth is ambition.[55] It next will be right
To describe each particular batch:
Distinguishing those that have feathers, and bite,
From those that have whiskers, and scratch.

---

52   Again our author links two words—"third" and "slowness" both have long
vowel sounds. Michael Everson disagrees ! He says: I can't hear a length
assonance in these words, but my dialect is different from Selwyn's, which
is certainly closer to Carroll's. What I do notice in this line is a prominence
of sibilants: "The third is its slowness in taking a jest", with its /z/, /ts/, /s/,
/s/, /st/. Compare similar sounds in "first" and "taste" /st/, /st/ (note 48)
and "chasms and crags" /k/, /z/, /z/, /k/, /g/, /z/ (note 41).

53   "fourth" and "fondness" are linked by their alliteration.

54   When I once gave a lecture to the Lewis Carroll Society of America, I
carried, and displayed, a number of bathing-machines—albeit small
ceramic models.

55   "is", "fifth", and "ambition" are all words with a short vowel /ɪ/—which fits
rather well with this very short mark,

"For, although common Snarks do no manner of harm,
   Yet I feel it my duty to say
Some are Boojums—" The Bellman broke off in alarm,
   For the Baker had fainted away.[56]

---

56   A highly dramatic moment, which will prove decisive in the saga.

Fit III
The Baker's Tale

The Baker's Tale

They roused him with muffins—they roused him with
    ice—
    They roused him with mustard and cress—
They roused him with jam and judicious advice—
    They set him conundrums to guess.[57]

When at length he sat up and was able to speak,
    His sad story he offered to tell;
And the Bellman cried "Silence! Not even a shriek!"[58]
    And excitedly tingled his bell.

---

57   The early rousing actions (three sets!) are just possible, though odd. The
last two one would have thought required the patient to be conscious, so
that the advice and conundrums can be heard.

58   Why did the Bellman expect shrieks?

There was silence supreme! Not a shriek, not a scream;
    Scarcely even a howl or a groan,
As the man they called "Ho!" told his story of woe[59]
    In an antediluvian tone.[60]   ①③Ⓑ

"My father and mother were honest, though poor—"
    "Skip all that!" cried the Bellman in haste.[61]
"If it once becomes dark, there's no chance of a
    Snark—
    We have hardly a minute to waste!"   ③Ⓑ

"I skip forty years," said the Baker, in tears,
    "And proceed without further remark
To the day when you took me aboard of your ship
    To help you in hunting the Snark.[62]   ①Ⓑ

---

59   *they called "Ho"*—actually this is not one of the nick names we were given in Fit I ('He would answer to 'Hi!' or to any loud cry')—perhaps used here as it rhymes rather conveniently with 'woe'.

60   *antediluvian*—masterly poetic use of the word.

61   *Skip all that!*—the Bellam is referring to the conventional start to a personal story.

62   Although he says 'the Snark', one assumes the initial invitation was to hunt for 'a Snark'.

"A dear uncle of mine (after whom I was named)[63]
    Remarked, when I bade him farewell—"
"Oh, skip your dear uncle!" the Bellman exclaimed,
    As he angrily tingled his bell.

"He remarked to me then," said that mildest of men,
    "'If your Snark be a Snark, that is right:
Fetch it home by all means—you may serve it with
    greens[64]
And it's handy for striking a light.[65]   ①⓭

"'You may seek it with thimbles—and seek it with care;
    You may hunt it with forks and hope;
You may threaten its life with a railway-share;
    You may charm it with smiles and soap—'"[66]

---

63   As usual in this saga, he may mention a name, but we are not told what it was.

64   These are further insights concerning the character of a Snark, adding to those listed above by the Bellman. Both statements are ambiguous. Is he suggesting that snark meat goes well with greens for consumption, or that you can serve greens as a dish for the Snark to consume?

65   As for "striking a light"—is he suggesting that about his person a Snark has either a tough hide (as suggested by Martin Gardner) or something like sandpaper on which he can strike a match, or is he simply saying that the Snark will assist in the process?

66   A key verse in the whole poem. We hear it again several times, though the wording varies slightly (see extended notes at the end of the poem). The advice is of course quite absurd, as befits the saga. Note the increasing ferocity of "seek", "hunt", "threaten" contrasting with "charm". The last two suggestions do imply a docile and attentive prey.

("That's exactly the method," the Bellman bold
　　In a hasty parenthesis cried,
"That's exactly the way I have always been told
　　That the capture of Snarks should be tried!")[67]

"'But oh, beamish nephew, beware of the day,[68]
　　If your Snark be a Boojum! For then
You will softly and suddenly vanish away,
　　And never be met with again!'

67　It is interesting that the Bellman agrees with the Baker's thoughts—
　　showing his knowledge of the life and activities of a Snark, though one
　　might have thought that he should have included these guidelines in his
　　earlier accounts of a Snark in Fit II.

68　*beamish*—Carroll uses a word first found in the poem Jabberwocky in
　　Through the Looking-Glass. Humpty Dumpty does not explain the word,
　　and it may not be original to Carroll.

"It is this, it is this that oppresses my soul,
　　When I think of my uncle's last words:
And my heart is like nothing so much as a bowl
　　Brimming over with quivering curds!⁶⁹

"It is this, it is this—" "We have had that before!"
　　The Bellman indignantly said.
And the Baker replied "Let me say it once more.
　　It is this, it is this that I dread!⁷⁰

"I engage with the Snark—every night after dark—
　　In a dreamy delirious fight:
I serve it with greens in those shadowy scenes,
　　And I use it for striking a light:⁷¹　　　　　①③🅱

69　The last two lines are an amusing yet vivid metaphor of timorous feelings.

70　Between this and the previous verse he says "it is this" six times—perhaps
　　emphasizing, by stating it twice each time (× 3), the Bellman's dictum that
　　"what I tell you three times is true".

71　These notions agree with his Uncle's suggestions above.

"But if ever I meet with a Boojum, that day,[72]
 In a moment (of this I am sure),
I shall softly and suddenly vanish away—
 And the notion I cannot endure!"[73]

---

72 We wait till this last verse, before understanding why the Baker fainted
    away at the end of Fit II.

73 We are never enlightened as to how you recognize if a Snark is a Boojum
    or not. Are there additional marks to show this? But see end of the poem.

Fit IV
The Hunting

The Hunting

The Bellman looked uffish, and wrinkled his brow.[74]
    "If only you'd spoken before!
It's excessively awkward to mention it now,
    With the Snark, so to speak, at the door!

"We should all of us grieve, as you well may believe,
    If you never were met with again—
But surely, my man, when the voyage began,
    You might have suggested it then?   ①③🅑

---

74   uffish—the second time in the poem that Carroll uses a word first found in
    "*Jabberwocky*" in Through the Looking-Glass. Humpty Dumpty does not
    explain the word, but The Annotated Snark explains: "in a letter to Maud
    Standen, Carroll said the word suggested to him 'a state of mind when the
    voice is gruffish, the manner roughish, and the temper huffish'."

"It's excessively awkward to mention it now—
  As I think I've already remarked."
And the man they called "Hi!" replied, with a sigh,
  "I informed you the day we embarked.   ③⑬

"You may charge me with murder—or want of sense—
  (We are all of us weak at times):[75]
But the slightest approach to a false pretence
  Was never among my crimes!

"I said it in Hebrew—I said it in Dutch—
  I said it in German and Greek:
But I wholly forgot (and it vexes me much)
  That English is what you speak!"

---

75   Whether a "charge of murder" is "weak" is surely a little doubtful, though
     the word may only refer to the second possibility.

"'Tis a pitiful tale," said the Bellman, whose face
    Had grown longer at every word:
"But, now that you've stated the whole of your case,
    More debate would be simply absurd.

"The rest of my speech" (he explained to his men)
    "You shall hear when I've leisure to speak it.
But the Snark is at hand, let me tell you again![76]
    'Tis your glorious duty to seek it!

"To seek it with thimbles, to seek it with care;
    To pursue it with forks and hope;
To threaten its life with a railway-share;
    To charm it with smiles and soap![77]

---

76   You might suggest that 'men' and 'again' are rhymes. But it is arguable.
    ME: The Oxford English Dictionary gives both /əˈgɛn/ and /əˈgeɪn/, in that
    order, for British English.

77   The second time this key verse is repeated.

"For the Snark's a peculiar creature, that wo'n't[78]
    Be caught in a commonplace way.
Do all that you know, and try all that you don't:
    Not a chance must be wasted to-day!

"For England expects—I forbear to proceed:
    'Tis a maxim tremendous, but trite:
And you'd best be unpacking the things that you need
    To rig yourselves out for the fight."[79]

---

78   The Bellman again refers to 'the Snark'—as if there is just the one, but
we know this is not true in view of the Bellman's previous statements.

79   The Bellman is of course quoting Nelson's words at the Battle of
Trafalgar: "England expects every man to do his duty."

Then the Banker[80] endorsed a blank cheque (which he
　　crossed),[81]
And changed his loose silver for notes:
The Baker with care combed his whiskers and hair,
　　And shook the dust out of his coats:　　③⑬

The Boots and the Broker were sharpening a spade—
　　Each working the grindstone in turn:
But the Beaver went on making lace, and displayed
　　No interest in the concern:[82]

Though the Barrister tried to appeal to its pride,
　　And vainly proceeded to cite
A number of cases, in which making laces
　　Had been proved an infringement of right.　　③⑬

80　As intimated above, the word "Banker" is misprinted as "Baker" in copies
　　of the Miniature edition of 1911. Unlike the earlier misprint (note 30
　　above) Macmillan tipped in an erratum slip correcting it. But the first
　　misprint remained throughout. I am grateful to Alan Tannenbaum who
　　first revealed these details see *Snarkologist* Vol.1, Fit 7.

81　If a cheque is crossed in Britain and Ireland—two parallel lines are added
　　across the cheque, and they denote that the cheque can only be paid into a
　　bank—that is, it cannot be "cashed" in any other way. It is a useful
　　precaution.

82　No interest in the concern—is he referring to the hunting, or the
　　sharpening of the spade? Martin Gardner has pointed out that we are given
　　no reason for the sharpening of the spade.

The maker of Bonnets ferociously planned
   A novel arrangement of bows:
While the Billiard-marker with quivering hand
   Was chalking the tip of his nose.

But the Butcher turned nervous, and dressed himself
      fine,
   With yellow kid gloves and a ruff—
Said he felt it exactly like going to dine,
   Which the Bellman declared was all "stuff."

"Introduce me, now there's a good fellow," he said,
   "If we happen to meet it together!"[83]
And the Bellman, sagaciously nodding his head,
   Said "That must depend on the weather."

---

83   Although later the Butcher explores with the Beaver, here it would seem he
     is thinking of going with the Bellman.

The Beaver went simply galumphing about,[84]
    At seeing the Butcher so shy:
And even the Baker, though stupid and stout,
    Made an effort to wink with one eye.

"Be a man!" said the Bellman in wrath, as he heard
    The Butcher beginning to sob.
"Should we meet with a Jubjub, that desperate bird,
    We shall need all our strength for the job!"

---

84   *galumphing*—another Carrollian word from "Jabberwocky". Although
never explained either by Humpty Dumpty or our Author, it would appear
to be a portmanteau word from "gallop" and "triumph".

Fit V
The Beaver's Lesson

The Beaver's Lesson

They sought it with thimbles, they sought it with care;
  They pursued it with forks and hope;
They threatened its life with a railway-share;
  They charmed it with smiles and soap.[85]

Then the Butcher contrived an ingenious plan
  For making a separate sally;
And had fixed on a spot unfrequented by man,
  A dismal and desolate valley.[86]

---

85   The third repetition of the key verse.

86   The last line is a brilliant alliterative phrase.

But the very same plan to the Beaver occurred:
    It had chosen the very same place:
Yet neither betrayed, by a sign or a word,
    The disgust that appeared in his face.

Each thought he was thinking of nothing but "Snark"
    And the glorious work of the day;
And each tried to pretend that he did not remark
    That the other was going that way.

But the valley grew narrow and narrower still,
    And the evening got darker and colder,
Till (merely from nervousness, not from good will)
    They marched along shoulder to shoulder.

Then a scream, shrill and high, rent the shuddering sky
    And they knew that some danger was near:
The Beaver turned pale to the tip of its tail,
    And even the Butcher felt queer.   ①③⑬

He thought of his childhood, left far far behind—
    That blissful and innocent state—
The sound so exactly recalled to his mind
    A pencil that squeaks on a slate!

"'Tis the voice of the Jubjub!" he suddenly cried.[87]
    (This man, that they used to call "Dunce.")[88]
"As the Bellman would tell you," he added with pride
    "I have uttered that sentiment once.

---

87   *the Jubjub*—as prophesied by the Bellman (see above) In *"Jabberwocky"*, there is no mention of the Jubjub's voice either shrill or high.

88   *"Dunce"*—this is the first mention of him being given the nickname 'Dunce' though it was previewed in note 27 (p. 16 above).

"'Tis the note of the Jubjub! Keep count, I entreat;
     You will find I have told it you twice.
'Tis the song of the Jubjub! The proof is complete,
     If only I've stated it thrice."[89]

The Beaver had counted with scrupulous care,
     Attending to every word:[90]
But it fairly lost heart, and outgrabe in despair,[91]
     When the third repetition occurred.

It felt that, in spite of all possible pains,
     It had somehow contrived to lose count,
And the only thing now was to rack its poor brains
     By reckoning up the amount.

---

89 Although indeed stated thrice, the description of the voice varies from
     "voice" to "note" to "song".

90 *every*—it is important when reciting the poem to pronounce each syllable,
     rather than say "ev'ry" as is more usual.

91 *outgrabe*—of course another Carrollian word from "*Jabberwocky*".

"Two added to one—if that could but be done,"
  It said, "with one's fingers and thumbs!"
Recollecting with tears how, in earlier years,
  It had taken no pains with its sums.[92]   ①③⑬

"The thing can be done," said the Butcher, "I think.[93]
  The thing must be done, I am sure.
The thing shall be done! Bring me paper and ink,[94]
  The best there is time to procure."

---

92   The Beaver tries to tackle the numbering in early stages.

93   It would seem that for the moment, the Butcher shares the Beaver's problems with sums.

94   The Butcher enjoys using different words concerning "thing"—i.e "the thing can be done" ... "must be done" ... "shall be done".

The Beaver brought paper, portfolio, pens,
    And ink in unfailing supplies:[95]
While strange creepy creatures came out of their dens,
    And watched them with wondering eyes.

So engrossed was the Butcher, he heeded them not,
    As he wrote with a pen in each hand,
And explained all the while in a popular style
    Which the Beaver could well understand.   ③🅑

"Taking Three as the subject to reason about—[96]
    A convenient number to state—
We add Seven, and Ten, and then multiply out
    By One Thousand diminished by Eight.[97]

---

95   There is something rather delightful in the way the Beaver is able suddenly
       to produce the necessary items. It is interesting that here, our Author uses
       an initial P for the items, contrasting with B for the crew members.

96   Taking three as the subject to reason about—confirms the Bellman's
       dictum "what I tell you three times is true".

97   So far: $(3 + 7 + 10) \times 992$.

"The result we proceed to divide, as you see,
　　By Nine-Hundred-and-Ninety-and-Two:[98]
Then subtract Seventeen, and the answer must be
　　Exactly and perfectly true.[99]

"The method employed I would gladly explain,
　　While I have it so clear in my head,
If I had but the time and you had but the brain—
　　But much yet remains to be said.[100]

"In one moment I've seen what has hitherto been
　　Enveloped in absolute mystery,
And without extra charge I will give you at large
　　A Lesson in Natural History."[101]　　　①③⑧

98　The hyphens were added in the second line when the poem was revised for the first reprint of *Rhyme? and Reason?*. They were retained in all English Macmillan editions till it went out of print after 1913.

99　The sum is of course very true—i.e $(((3 + 7 + 10) \times 992) \div 992) - 17 = 3$. Is interesting the way our Author has made the sums appear more complicated than they actually are— by altering the way it is set out. So— 'three... we add seven and ten.' In in the second half of the sum this is stated as 'seventeen'—it sounds different but is of course the same. Similarly with—'multiply out by One Thousand diminished by Eight'. In the second half of the sum this is stated as 'divide... by Nine-Hundred-and-Ninety-and-Two'—again this sounds different, but is of course the same.

100　Quite what remains to be said is not vouchsafed to us.

101　It would appear that the Butcher not only convinces the Beaver of his solution, but recognizes its brilliance himself.

In his genial way he proceeded to say
  (Forgetting all laws of propriety,
And that giving instruction, without introduction,
  Would have caused quite a thrill in Society), ①③⑬

"As to temper the Jubjub's a desperate bird,[102]
  Since it lives in perpetual passion:[103]
Its taste in costume is entirely absurd—
  It is ages ahead of the fashion:[104]

"But it knows any friend it has met once before:
  It never will look at a bribe:
And in charity-meetings it stands at the door,
  And collects—though it does not subscribe.

---

102 Having dealt with the mathematical problems created by hearing the Jubjub's cry, the Butcher can now return to the matter in hand—i.e. discussion on the Jubjub.

103 *perpetual passion*—another example of a brilliant alliterative phrase, and again employing P as the initial letter.

104 We learn more about the Jubjub—far more than we ever learnt from "Jabberwocky".

"Its flavour when cooked is more exquisite far
Than mutton, or oysters, or eggs:[105]
(Some think it keeps best in an ivory jar,
And some, in mahogany kegs:)

"You boil it in sawdust: you salt it in glue:
You condense it with locusts and tape:
Still keeping one principal object in view—
To preserve its symmetrical shape."[106]

The Butcher would gladly have talked till next day,
But he felt that the Lesson must end,
And he wept with delight in attempting to say
He considered the Beaver his friend:

105　The assonance in the first two lines shows a subtle interveaving of vowel
sounds.

106　Our Author enjoys relating absurd methods of cooking—the Butcher's
ideas remind us of the White Knight's pudding—which included blotting
paper, gunpowder, and sealing wax.

While the Beaver confessed, with affectionate looks
    More eloquent even than tears,
It had learned in ten minutes far more than all books
    Would have taught it in seventy years.

They   returned   hand-in-hand,   and   the   Bellman,
    unmanned
    (For a moment) with noble emotion,
Said "This amply repays all the wearisome days
    We have spent on the billowy ocean!"   ①③❸

Such friends, as the Beaver and Butcher became,
    Have seldom if ever been known;
In winter or summer, 'twas always the same—
    You could never meet either alone.

And when quarrels arose—as one frequently finds
    Quarrels will, spite of every endeavour—[107]
The song of the Jubjub recurred to their minds,
    And cemented their friendship for ever!

---

107 *spite of*—this really needs expanding to 'in spite of' but that would damage
the metre.

Fit VI
The Barrister's Dream

The Barrister's Dream

They sought it with thimbles, they sought it with care;
    They pursued it with forks and hope;
They threatened its life with a railway-share;
    They charmed it with smiles and soap.[108]

But the Barrister, weary of proving in vain
    That the Beaver's lace-making was wrong,
Fell asleep, and in dreams saw the creature quite plain
    That his fancy had dwelt on so long.

---

108   The fourth repetition of this verse.

He dreamed that he stood in a shadowy Court,
 Where the Snark, with a glass in its eye,
Dressed in gown, bands, and wig, was defending a pig
 On the charge of deserting its sty.   ③⓭

The Witnesses proved, without error or flaw,
 That the sty was deserted when found:
And the Judge kept explaining the state of the law
 In a soft under-current of sound.

The indictment had never been clearly expressed,
 And it seemed that the Snark had begun,
And had spoken three hours, before any one guessed
 What the pig was supposed to have done.

The Jury had each formed a different view
(Long before the indictment was read),
And they all spoke at once, so that none of them knew
One word that the others had said.

"You must know—" said the Judge: but the Snark
exclaimed "Fudge!
That statute is obsolete quite!
Let me tell you, my friends, the whole question depends
On an ancient manorial right.[109]   ①③⑱

"In the matter of Treason the pig would appear[110]
To have aided, but scarcely abetted:
While the charge of Insolvency fails, it is clear,
If you grant the plea 'never indebted.'

---

109   *That statute is obsolete*—we have to understand from the punctuation that
this is a continuation of the Snark's defence speech, and not spoken by the
Judge. We are not told what statute the Snark is referring to. Nor are we
given any indication of what the Judge was beginning to say.

110   What treason, one wonders.

"The fact of Desertion I will not dispute:
But its guilt, as I trust, is removed
(So far as relates to the costs of this suit)
By the Alibi which has been proved.[111]

"My poor client's fate now depends on your votes."
Here the speaker sat down in his place,
And directed the Judge to refer to his notes
And briefly to sum up the case.

But the Judge said he never had summed up before;[112]
So the Snark undertook it instead,
And summed it so well that it came to far more
Than the Witnesses ever had said!

---

111 *the Alibi*—presumable provided by "the witnesses" in verse 4.

112 For a Judge to have attained that position, his assertion that he has never "summed up before" seems a little strange as all court lawyers will have had lots of experience of summing up—before being raised to being a judge.

When the verdict was called for, the Jury declined,
   As the word was so puzzling to spell;[113]
But they ventured to hope that the Snark wouldn't
   mind
   Undertaking that duty as well.

So the Snark found the verdict, although, as it owned,
   It was spent with the toils of the day:
When it said the word "GUILTY!"[114] the Jury all
   groaned,
   And some of them fainted away.[115]

Then the Snark pronounced sentence, the Judge being
   quite
   Too nervous to utter a word:
When it rose to its feet, there was silence like night,
   And the fall of a pin might be heard.

---

113 What word was puzzling to spell?

114 The Snark has been the defence lawyer, so his verdict seems rather
surprising.

115 And the behaviour of the Jury is also surprising, they should not react in
any way to a court verdict.

"Transportation for life" was the sentence it gave,
  "And *then* to be fined forty pound."[116]
The Jury all cheered,[117] though the Judge said he
    feared
  That the phrase was not legally sound.   ③ ⑬

But their wild exultation was suddenly checked
  When the jailer informed them, with tears,
Such a sentence would have not the slightest effect,
  As the pig had been dead for some years.

The Judge left the Court, looking deeply disgusted:[118]
  But the Snark, though a little aghast,
As the lawyer to whom the defence was intrusted,
  Went bellowing on to the last.[119]

---

116 *forty pound*—this really should be "forty pounds"—but that would not
    rhyme with "sound" in line 4.

117 Again a jury should not react to court decisions, and although the Judge
    comments on the phrase not being sound, he does not argue about it.

118 *deeply disgusted*—another example of a brilliant alliterative phrase.

119 Quite what he bellowed about we are never told.

Thus the Barrister dreamed, while the bellowing seemed

To grow every moment more clear:

Till he woke to the knell of a furious bell,
Which the Bellman rang close at his ear.[120]   ③ ⓑ

---

120   We are not told why the Bellman rang the bell so furiously—was he simply trying to wake the Barrister up from his dream?

Fit VII
The Banker's Fate

The Banker's Fate

They sought it with thimbles, they sought it with care;
    They pursued it with forks and hope;
They threatened its life with a railway-share;
    They charmed it with smiles and soap.[121]

And the Banker, inspired with a courage so new
    It was matter for general remark,
Rushed madly ahead and was lost to their view
    In his zeal to discover the Snark.[122]

---

121   The fifth repetition of this verse.

122   the Snark—again we have this slight problem. Are they in fact hunting a
particular snark—or just any snark?

But while he was seeking with thimbles and care,
    A Bandersnatch swiftly drew nigh[123]
And grabbed at the Banker, who shrieked in despair,
    For he knew it was useless to fly.

He offered large discount—he offered a cheque
    (Drawn "to bearer") for seven-pounds-ten:
But the Bandersnatch merely extended its neck
    And grabbed at the Banker again.

Without rest or pause—while those frumious jaws[124]
    Went savagely snapping around—[125]
He skipped and he hopped, and he floundered and
    flopped,
    Till fainting he fell to the ground.[126]

---

123 *Bandersnatch*—another creature from *"Jabberwocky"*. We know from
Through the Looking-Glass, that Bandersnatches are swift:

    "Would you—be good enough——" Alice panted out, after
running a little further, "to stop a minute—just to get—one's
breath again?"

    "I'm good enough," the King said, "only I'm not strong enough.
You see, a minute goes by so fearfully quick. You might just as
well try to stop a Bandersnatch!"

124 frumious—another portmanteau word from "Jabberwocky". The word is
not explained by Humpty Dumpty, but our Author does—in the preface to
this very poem (see above).

125 A verse with two fine examples of brilliant alliterative phrases.

126 Fainting is a recurrent feature of the whole saga—from the Baker in Fit
III, to some of the Jury in Fit VI to the Banker here.

The Bandersnatch fled as the others appeared
    Led on by that fear-stricken yell:[127]
And the Bellman remarked "It is just as I feared!"
    And solemnly tolled on his bell.

He was black in the face, and they scarcely could trace
    The least likeness to what he had been:
While so great was his fright that his waistcoat turned
       white—
    A wonderful thing to be seen!   ①③🅑

To the horror of all who were present that day,
    He uprose in full evening dress,
And with senseless grimaces endeavoured to say
    What his tongue could no longer express.

---

127   The fear-stricken yell was from the Banker (see above).

Down he sank in a chair—ran his hands through his
    hair—
And chanted in mimsiest[128] tones
Words whose utter inanity proved his insanity,
    While he rattled a couple of bones.   ①③⑬

"Leave him here to his fate—it is getting so late!"
    The Bellman exclaimed in a fright.
"We have lost half the day. Any further delay,
    And we sha'n't catch a Snark before night!"   ①③

---

128   mimsiest—another use of a portmanteau neologism from "*Jabberwocky*",
explained by Humpty Dumpty as being from "flimsy" and "miserable".

Fit VIII
The Vanishing

FIT THE EIGHTH

The Vanishing

They sought it with thimbles, they sought it with care;
  They pursued it with forks and hope;
They threatened its life with a railway-share;
  They charmed it with smiles and soap.[129]

They shuddered to think that the chase might fail,
  And the Beaver, excited at last,
Went bounding along on the tip of its tail,
  For the daylight was nearly past.

---

129 The sixth repetition of this verse.

"There is Thingumbob shouting!" the Bellman said,
  "He is shouting like mad, only hark!
He is waving his hands, he is wagging his head,
  He has certainly found a Snark!"

They gazed in delight, while the Butcher exclaimed
  "He was always a desperate wag!"[130]
They beheld him—their Baker—their hero unnamed—
  On the top of a neighbouring crag,

Erect and sublime, for one moment of time,
  In the next, that wild figure they saw
(As if stung by a spasm) plunge into a chasm,
  While they waited and listened in awe.   ①③⑬

---

130 The Butcher we know is fond of words, and here he expresses two meanings
     of the word "wag"—the shaking of the head, and the expression about a
     witty person.

"It's a Snark!" was the sound that first came to their
   ears,
And seemed almost too good to be true.[131]
Then followed a torrent of laughter and cheers:
   Then the ominous words "It's a Boo—"

Then, silence. Some fancied they heard in the air
   A weary and wandering sigh[132]
That sounded like "—jum!" but the others declare
   It was only a breeze that went by.

---

131 It would appear that though he was so delighted to have found the Snark,
     the realization that it was a Boojum was slightly delayed.

132 *weary and wandering*—another brilliant alliterative phrase.

They hunted till darkness came on, but they found
    Not a button, or feather, or mark,
By which they could tell that they stood on the ground
    Where the Baker had met with the Snark.

In the midst of the word he was trying to say,
    In the midst of his laughter and glee,
He had softly and suddenly vanished away—
    For the Snark was a Boojum, you see.[133]

---

133   you see—this is the only time that our Author addresses the reader
directly, unlike the Alice books where it is a regular feature.

    This is the last verse, so we never learn if the rest of the crew were
successful, after hunting for buttons or feathers or marks, in capturing the
Snark. It seems a little doubtful as it was some distance away from them
at the time of the Baker's vanishing.

Notes on the key verse

FIT III VERSE 8

"'You may seek it with thimbles—and seek it with care;
　　You may hunt it with forks and hope;
You may threaten its life with a railway-share;
　　You may charm it with smiles and soap—'"[134]

FIT IV VERSE 8

To seek it with thimbles, to seek it with care;
　　To pursue it with forks and hope;
To threaten its life with a railway-share;
　　To charm it with smiles and soap![135]

134　The verse is repeated five times, though the wording differs slightly in the
　　first three renderings.
135　Note the change from "you may seek it" to "to seek it". The additional loss
　　of "and" at the end of the line makes the whole line shorter. There is also
　　a change of "you may" to "to" in the last three lines. Curiously "hunt" in
　　line 2 is changed to "pursue". The advice is not quite as aggressive as the
　　first rendering.

FIT V VERSE 1

They sought it with thimbles, they sought it with care;
They pursued it with forks and hope;
They threatened its life with a railway-share;
They charmed it with smiles and soap.[136]

---

136 Note the change of tense throughout from "to seek" to "they sought"; from "to pursue" to "they pursued"; from "to threaten" to "they threatened"; from "to charm" to "they charmed"—all displaying a more personal involvement by the crew, as the advice truns into practical details.

The advice is of course quite absurd, as befits the saga. Note the increasing ferocity of "seek", "hunt" (or "pursue"), "threaten" contrasting with "charm". The last two suggestions do imply a docile and attentive prey.

The last three repetitions of the verse (Fit VI verse 1, Fit VII verse 1, and Fit VIII, verse 1) all follow the second revision as in Fit V verse 1.

The Listing of the Snark

"...go on with your list..."
(*Through the Looking-Glass*, 1871)

*T*he origin of this section is a booklet I issued on the centenary of the Snark inspiration, on 18 July 1974. Subsequently this was developed into the section included in the 1981 centennial edition of *The Hunting of the Snark*, published by William Kaufmann, Inc. I updated it for the 2006 *Annotated Snark* edition and now it is again brought up to date with a few notable additions.

I am once more indebted to my fellow collectors and enthusiasts who have greatly assisted me in supplying me with details of copies in their possession, and for their further helpful and constructive criticism. In particular I must thank Sandor and Mark Burstein, Joel Birenbaum, August and Clare Imholtz, Charlie Lovett, Yoshiyuka Momma, Mark and Catherine Richards, David Schaefer, Byron Sewell, Alan Tannenbaum, and Edward Wakeling. I am also most grateful to Michael Everson (the publisher of this book) for his enormous help and for providing numerous additions to the list of editions, translation, and 'candle-ends'.

The listing is in five sections: English-language editions, translations, anthologies including the entire *Snark*, theatrical and musical adaptations and recordings, and "candle-ends". The entries are arranged chronologically, but each edition is pursued to its final disappearance, even if the chase extends over forty-two years. Where a description appears meagre and hollow, it simply means that darkness came on before a copy was run to earth.

I thank my fellow members of various Snark clubs, in particular the famous Cambridge Snark Club, which finally allowed me to join its illustrious ranks in 1994 as "Boots III", and who annually shudder to think that the chase might fail.

English-Language Editions

1876 Macmillan, London. The first edition, published on 29 March. Dodgson's own copy was dated 30 March 1876, but he inscribed eighty copies for presentation on 29 March. He had earlier thought it would be published on 1 April: "Surely that is the fittest day for it to appear."

The book is fully described in *The Lewis Carroll Handbook* (revised version by Denis Crutch, 1979), but there are two minor errors of description: on the title page, the comma after GLASS should be a full stop; and the lettering on the spine has stops before THE and after SNARK (as well as between each word).

The basic binding is buff cloth boards (which by now are usually found "weathered" to grey). Dodgson arranged for a number of copies to be bound in special covers: on 21 March 1876 he asked for 100 in red and gold..., 20 in dark blue and gold, 20 in dark green and gold, 2 in white vellum and gold." In 1877 he offered a child-friend the choice of light blue or light green.

Edward Wakeling and I have compiled a list of presentation copies and copies in special bindings and this has been recently updated by Catherine Richards and myself—fully detailed in *The Snarkologist* Vol. 1 Fit 5, April 2023. At the present count there are 58 inscribed red copies, and at least 22 red copies, with no author inscription which raises the strong possibility that a number of red cloth copies of the first edition were on sale to the general public, possibly as a deluxe alternative to the regular buff cloth.

We have records of 29 blue cloth copies, one in green, and 29 in dark bluish-green (some of these are recorded as "dark green" and some "dark blue"—but it is nearly impossible to say which is which, so we have listed them together). Two copies are recorded as in "white vellum", and a further eight simply as in white cloth. We know of eight copies with inscriptions later than 29 March 1876, and 14 copies where the colour and edition are not known.

A number of "curiosities" are known—the Harcourt Amory Catalogue (Harvard University) records a copy in "tan cloth, lettered and ornamented in black", and comments that a lavender colour is also known. There is known to be a presentation copy in blue and gilt, which has the bell and sail only, on the front cover, with bell buoy on the back.

Four copies are known in dust jackets. Two of the copies are in red cloth, two in the standard buff. The front cover of the jacket has a reproduction of the title page; the spine has the title in roman uppercase, lettered upward; the back cover has the Macmillan advertisements for books by Lewis Carroll; and the text on both covers is within a line frame around the border.

The first edition consisted of ten thousand copies, and many are found with *An Easter Greeting* (issued Easter 1876) loosely inserted. It is possible that all copies originally had them. Easter Sunday in 1876 was on 16 April.

We know of four copies of the first edition in a red "Alice-style" cloth (the Alice roundels on front and back covers are replaced by the Bellman on the front and Beaver on the back), This was also used (see below) for copies of the 18th thousand 1876 and some copies of the 17th thousand 1876. One copy, at least, of the 13th thousand is also known in this "Alice-style" cloth.

Early reprints have the number of "thousand" on the title page. The first reprint was in May 1876. Copies are identical to the first edition, apart from respacing on the title page to accommodate the number of thousand (below **HENRY HOLIDAY**) in thick black lowercase. Copies have been seen with "Eleventh", "Twelfth", "Thirteenth", "Fourteenth", and "Fifteenth".

The second reprint was in December 1876. Copies now have the number of thousand in uppercase italics, in the same position. The reprint includes the "Sixteenth", "Seventeenth", and "Eighteenth" thousands. During the issue of this reprint, the binding style changed from the buff cloth to the red "Alice-style" cloth as detailed above. Copies of the "seventeenth" thousand are known in both styles. The price rose from 3/6 to 4/6 in 1877 probably coincidental with the change in binding.

Stocks remained available for sale until 1883, when they were withdrawn because of the publication of *Rhyme? And Reason?* (which included the full text and pictures of the *Snark*).

In 1890 the *Snark* was readvertised. Remaining bound copies of the "Eighteenth Thousand" were sold off first. The new issue was bound in red cloth boards, decorated and lettered in gilt in a return to the pictorial design of the first edition. The first issue, styled "Nineteenth Thousand", appeared in July 1890. Thereafter the date of reprint appears on the reverse of the title page—the first in December 1890. Reprints followed in 1891, 1893, 1894, 1895, and 1896. For the first reprint of 1897, the height was increased slightly (from 18.5 to 18.7 cm) to match the similar increase in height of the new editions of the Alice books of 1897.

Reprints followed in 1897, 1898, 1899, 1900, 1903 (when the endpapers changed from black to white), 1906, 1908, and 1910. Advertisements in other Carroll works give varying numbers of thousand for the edition as the years go by, but no great reliance can be placed on these numbers. For example, "20th Thousand" is quoted in 1897 and also in 1908, whereas other 1908 advertisements state "25th Thousand".

The price remained at 4/6 until 1918 when it rose to 6/–. The edition finally went out of print in 1920, just over forty-two years after it was first published.

Many of the reprints will have had dust jackets, but examples are rare. A 1908 reprint example has been seen: a speckled yellow paper covered with a close design based on the Macmillan motif in orange. The title is in black, with an elaborate Macmillan motif in black in the center; title, etc., on the spine; and the back with the advertisements, flaps blank.

1876 James R. Osgood, Boston. A curious production, presumably pirated, and probably produced by a photographic process from a copy of the English edition, which it mimics closely apart from being very small. Buff paperboards, paler yellow end papers. Pp. xiv, 86. 13.2 × 8.6 cm. Reprinted in 1877.

1890 Macmillan, New York. Possibly timed to coincide with the new reprint in England. The binding is similar to the English edition—red cloth—but the pictures and lettering are in black. Reprinted in 1891.

(1896) A. L. Burt, New York. In copies of *Through the Looking-Glass*, in The Little Women Series and The Wellesley Series for Girls, the *Snark* appears on pp. 183–226.

1897 Van Vechten & Ellis, Wausau, Wisconsin. A limited edition of ninety-nine numbered copies. Vellum boards, decorated in red and black; dredges uncut. The text is printed in black with wide red decorative borders. William H. Ellis contributes "A Word by Way of Palliation", "Explanatory Diagrams and Picturings by Gardner C. Teall". This fine volume was the second book to be issued by the

Philosopher Press, "finished on this ninth day of June" but published in November.

There is a cheaper edition, issued at the same time, limited to 333 numbered copies. Beige paperboards, title, etc., and picture within a frame in dark brown on both covers. The text lacks the wide decorative borders. Pp. 88. 15.6 × 12 cm.

1898 Macmillan, New York. Plain red cloth boards, title in gilt on the spine reading up. The covers have a single line around the border in blind. All edges plain, white endpapers, no advertisements. Printed on one side of the leaf only; 52 leaves. The setup of type is from *Rhyme? And Reason?*. 18.6 × 12.3 cm.

Reprinted in 1899, 1902 (when the title on the spine reads down), 1908, 1914 (the copy examined is in green cloth, with title and design on front in white, a white line round the border, title, etc., on spine in white, back blank; this may be a variant), 1922, 1923, 1927, 1930 (the copy seen has title and author on front cover in blind), and 1937. Thus, just about forty-two years in print.

1899 A. L. Burt, New York. The *Snark* occupies pp. 1–48 (with the Holiday illustrations), and selections from *Sylvie and Bruno* occupy pp. 49–206. Pp. 206 plus two leaves and advertisements. Possibly reprinted in 1910, but no details available.

1903 Harper and Bros., New York and London. Full title *The Hunting of the Snark & Other Poems and Verses*. Illustrations by Peter Newell in sepia monochrome, frontispiece in colour. Cream vellum boards, decorated and lettered in gilt; embossed gilt Bellman on the lower front cover. Top edge gilt, others uncut. The *Snark* is on pp. 5–41, with eight pictures (including the frontispiece). The text pages have a wide decorative border in pale green, by Robert Murray Wright.

Issued in a green dust jacket, with the same design on the front as the front cover; possibly originally issued in a cloth board slipcase, in quarter vellum with gilt title. The Harcourt Amory Catalogue, apparently describing this edition, suggests that it should be enclosed in an oilpaper jacket lettered on the spine, with "Price $3.00 net". Pp. xiv, 248. 22 × 14.5 cm.

There are two other issues—in green ribbed cloth boards and in red cloth boards.

It seems likely that there was also an issue to match the Peter Newell Edition of the Alice books—black cloth boards with paste-on colour picture and title on the front cover. This could be the 1906 reprint. Another issue was in the Harper's Young People Series, 1903. Green cloth boards with title and figure in red, within decorated border of characters; text printed without ornamental borders; 17.3 × 12 cm. "There was also an issue in blue cloth boards, lettered in dark blue; 16.8 × 11.8 cm. Another issue is in green boards, but not in the Young People Series.

1906 G. P. Putman & Sons, Knickerbocker Press, New York and London. In the series Ariel Booklets. Limp red leather with title in gilt within an ornamental surround; gilt ornamentation also around the border; back blank, the spine with the title, etc., in gilt. Includes the Holiday illustrations (which are attributed to Swain!); also includes poems from the Alice books (with Tenniel pictures) and from other works. Pp. xi, 124. 13.8 × 9.5 cm.

1909 Altemus, Philadelphia. In the Slip-in-the-Pocket Classics series and listed in the *Publishers' Trade List Annual* for 1909–13, 1916, and 1921, although actual copies simply give the copyright date of 1909. A floral design frames the cover design; the series name is printed on the front cover and spine of the dust jacket. Bindings vary; one is known with a paste-on picture of a landscape signed "J. C. Claghorn". Another copy has been seen in green cloth boards, title and author on the front cover in gilt in an elaborate floral design, title on the spine in gilt, back blank. Pp. 120 plus three blank leaves at the front and two at the back. 13.1 × 10.2 cm.

Also known in the Langhorne Series—"Velvet Calf, Gilt top, Boxed, 75c".

1910 Macmillan, London. The Miniature Edition, published in October, in the same format as the Miniature Editions of the Alice books (1907 and 1908). Red cloth boards, the front cover with the Bellman roundel in gilt, a little above center; the back cover is blank; the three parallel lines around the borders are in blind, but in gilt on the spine; title and publisher in gilt on the spine. Issued in a dust jacket, very similar in design to the examples found on some of the contemporary reprints of the standard edition (see above)—speckled yellow paper covered with a close design in orange based on the Macmillan motif, with lettering in black; the back cover has the advertisements; flaps blank. Pp. xiv, 84, leaf with advertisements. 15.4 × 9.9 cm.

Reprinted in November 1910, 1911, 1913, 1916, 1920, 1924, 1928, 1931, and 1935. The first-edition style of dust jacket was retained at least until the 1916 reprint. The 1931 reprint dust jacket is in blue on a white paper; the front cover has the Bellman roundel, the back the advertisements, the flaps blank. The dust jacket for the 1935 reprint is in red on white; the front cover has the illustration for the Baker's Tale, the back is blank, the front flap has the advertisements, the back flap is blank.

As with the standard edition, no great reliance can be placed on the number of thousand stated in the various advertisements. In November 1910 it reads "10th thousand", 1911 "15th thousand", 1913 "20th thousand"; by 1918 it is consistently "20th thousand", but thereafter the number is no longer stated.

The price of the first edition was is. In 1918 it rose to 1/6; in 1921 to 2s; in 1942 to 2/6. It was last advertised in 1948, four years short of forty-two years in print.

The 1928 issue was the first where an alternative binding was offered—écrasé morocco, at 5s. This is in blue morocco with covers blank; title, etc., on the spine in gilt. The 1928 and subsequent issues were also offered in "ledura leather cloth", at 3s (rising to 3/6 in 1942). This is yellow, with the same roundel in gilt with three slightly elaborated yellow bands in blind around. Title, etc., on the spine in gilt, with embossed ship, back blank.

It seems likely that the ledura versions were issued in a glassine "transmatic" dust jacket; these consist of a transparent plastic jacket with printed paper flaps. It appears to be a Macmillan invention, as examples of the 1928 transmatic jacket have a printed note "patent appl'd for"; later examples have a patent number.

(1927) **Kahoe and Spieth, Yellow Springs, Ohio.** Unillustrated. Marbled paperboards, with paper label on spine with title in black. Pp. vi, 58 (last three leaves blank). 17.3 × 11 cm.

(1932) **Peter Pauper Press, New Rochelle, New York.** Illustrated by Edward A. Wilson. Green, beige, and brown decorated paperboards, green cloth spine with title and motifs in gilt. A limited issue of 275 unnumbered copies, printed at the Walpole Printing Office on a green-tinted paper. A picture begins each fit and has block coloring, the colour changing for each fit. Pp. 80. 25.1 × 15.7 cm.

A single-leaf prospectus was issued, printed on the same green paper and carrying one of the pictures. 25.1 × 15.9 cm.

Undated (c.1930s?) Haldeman-Julius Company, Girard, Kansas. Number 989 in the series Little Blue Books, edited by E. Haldeman-Julius. Unillustrated. Pale blue paper jacket, lettered in black, Pp. 32. 12.5 × 8.7 cm.

(1939) Peter Pauper Press, Mount Vernon, New York. Illustrated by Cobbledick. Decorated green paperboards; issued in a slipcase. Pictorial title page in green, sepia, and black. Each page is decorated in green and sepia. Pp. 75. 19.5 × 14.0 cm.

There is another issue, also undated. Limited to 1,450 unnumbered copies. Grey paperboards, with darker grey postage-stamp-size illustrations of the characters. Black on red paper label on the spine with the title. Bottom edges uncut. Pictorial title page in red, grey, and black. Each page decorated, the colors changing in rotation for each fit—grey/red; grey/green; grey/orange; grey/blue. Issued in a red paperboards slipcase. Pp. 78. 20.1 × 13.5 cm.

1939 Oxford University Press, London. Full title *The Hunting of the Snark and Other Verses.* Number 2 in the series Chameleon Books. Unillustrated, but the black front endpapers carry a picture of seven of the crew in black line on white, coloured with brown, and the back endpaper Alice and characters from the Alice books, both by Malcolm Easton. Paperboards decorated with a design of fish in brown and grey; title, etc., in grey on the front cover and spine. Issued in matching dust jacket; the title here is given as *The Hunting of the Snark & Other Lewis Carroll Verses.* The other verses are from the Alice books and *Sylvie and Bruno.* Pp. 64. 18 × 12.4 cm.

Reprinted in 1946 (where the first edition is said to be 1940) and 1949.

1941 Chatto & Windus, London. Illustrated by Mervyn Peake. Yellow paperboards, the front cover reproducing in black the title and picture from p. 19, the back cover the illustration from p. 26, with title above and refrain verse and publisher below; title on the spine in black.

Number 26 in the series Zodiac Books. Published on 20 November 1941, at 1s. Pp. 48. 18 × 11.3 cm.

Second impression, 1941. Pink cloth boards, with title on the spine in gilt. Issued in a grey dust jacket, which repeats on the front the title-page design but without the date; the back has the p. 40 illustration enlarged, with publisher's name. Title, etc., on the spine. 20.8 × 13 cm. The text and pictures are identical to the first edition, except for the title page where both are increased in size. This deluxe issue was published on 16 December 1941, at 5s; 1,400 unnumbered copies were printed.

Third impression, 1942. Styled "Second Impression" (on the title page reverse).

Fourth impression, 1948. Very similar to the first, but no mention of previous issues. Published by Lighthouse Books Ltd. and distributed by Chatto & Windus. On p. [47] the *Snark* is listed as Number 4 in a list of six titles in the series Zodiac Books. Name of publisher is removed from the back cover; price "2s." added.

Fifth impression, 1953. Styled "Fourth Impression". Blank yellow paperboards simulating cloth, with title and publisher's device on the spine in gilt. Issued in a dust jacket that copies the binding of the first edition, but with nothing below the refrain on the back. 18.5 × 12.3 cm.

Sixth impression, 1958. Styled "Fifth Impression".

Seventh impression, 1960. A special issue for the Reprint Society Book Club. Slightly smaller than the 1953 and ensuing impressions— 18.2 × 12.2 cm. The reverse of the title page has "This edition published by the Reprint Society Ltd. by arrangement with Chatto & Windus Ltd. 1960". Limp beige cloth. Front cover has in black the title, author, illustrator, and part of the p. 45 illustration; back cover has the title, etc., and p. 10 illustration, with note of the Book Society.

Eighth impression, 1964. Styled "Sixth Impression". As the sixth, with price (5s. net) added on the front flap of the dust jacket.

Ninth impression, 1969. Styled "Fourth Impression", but giving a list of impressions from 1953; standard book number added and also on the front flap with the new price (10/– net 50p).

Tenth impression, 1973. Styled "Fifth Impression", but including a bibliographical listing back to the first edition of 1941. Date deleted from title page.

Eleventh impression, 1975. Styled "Sixth Impression". There is a note at the bottom of the tile page reverse that the illustrations are "c Maeve Peake 1941". The dust jacket has the title running down the front free edge, with note of illustrator at the bottom left. The front flap has the title and illustrator, picture of the Beaver, and price change to 70p net.

Twelfth impression, 1981. Styled "Seventh Impression". Price change to £1.95 net.

"Eighth", "ninth", "tenth" impressions not seen.

"Eleventh impression", 1988. Blue paperboards in a blue dust jacket, with new design.

Pocket Library, 1993. Glazed paperboards, yellow cloth spine. 14.4 × 11.6 cm. No price stated.

Reissue 2000, with suite of working drawings. Maroon paperboards, lettered in spine in silver. In dust jacket. Pp. 70. 19.9 × 12.6 cm. Price £9.99.

(1952) Peter Pauper Press, and Mayflower Publishing Co., and Vision Press, New York. The cover title is *The Hunting of the Snark, and Other Nonsense Verse*; the other verses are from the Alice books and *Sylvie and Bruno*. Illustrations by Aldren Watson. There appear to be two issues of this volume. The standard edition has a picture at the head of each fit in green. Bound in yellow paperboards, with a fish design, title on upper half of front cover in yellow oblong in a frame; title on spine in yellow on pink; issued in a blue-green slipcase with yellow label with title, etc., and extra picture in green. Pp. 92, 22.4 × 13.6 cm. Also issued as a Collector's Presentation Edition (not seen).

1962 Simon & Schuster, New York (also issued by Bramhall House). *The Annotated Snark*, introduction and notes by Martin Gardner. Buff half-cloth, dark brown paperboards, with gilt bell on the lower front cover, spine lettered in brown. Cream dust jacket, with title, etc., in red, black, and brown, all within a frame of the Bellman's map. The back has laudatory extracts from reviews of *The Annotated Alice*. Pp. 112. 25 × 14.8 cm.

This book, which contains the full text, copious annotations, bibliography, Holiday illustrations, and appendixes, has been rightly called the "apotheosis of Snarkolatry". The 1981 Kaufmann edition and the 2006 edition are the revised and augmented developments of this book (for details, see below).

First published in England by Penguin Books Ltd., London, 1967. It contains a new preface by Martin Gardner, the entire book revised, updated, and new material added. Paper jackets, with a pictorial cover designed by Germano Facetti, using six of the Holiday illustrations. The back cover has a two-verse parody about the book.

Reprinted in 1973, with revisions and extended bibliography. Also new jackets designed by David Pelham, in pale blue featuring on the front cover in brown the title and the Holiday picture of the Bellman supporting the Banker, the upper half against a turquoise circle; the back cover has the same circle, with parody and text as before. Reprinted in 1975 (where it states that the 1973 reprint was in 1974) and again in 1977, and 1979 with further small corrections. And in 1984 (where the 1974 reprint is said to be 1980), and again in 1987. Reprinted several times with the 1974 date and changes in coding. Reissued in 1995 with a new design as part of Penguin Classics, and subsequent changes in coding.

1966 Pantheon Books, New York. Illustrations by Kelly Oechsli, in line from pen-and-ink drawings, with added colour wash. Black half-cloth, buff paperboard; title on the spine in grey. Dust jacket in white, with an extra picture on the front cover against a blue background of the ship in sail approaching; the back cover has the ship viewed sailing away. Pp. iii, 48. 25.5 × 17.5 cm.

1966 De Roos, Utrecht. Illustrations by Peter Vos. An edition specially prepared for members of De Roos, Utrecht, limited to 175 numbered copies on paper made by Hahnemuhle, bound by Proost and Brandt, n.v. Amsterdam. Paperboards with illustrations in monochrome extending over both covers; title on spine in silver. All edges plain. Pp. 40. 25.3 × 17.2 cm.

1968 Manus Press, Stuttgart. Eleven lithographs in colour, seven hors-texte; one in black and ten in negative by Max Ernst. Portfolio, in publisher's slipcase. Limited to thirty-three signed copies with an extra suite of twelve signed and numbered lithographs on Japon, and 130 copies signed and numbered on Papier Arches (no extra suite). Pp. 100. Copies of this astonishing tour de force fetch huge prices on the rare occasions they reach auction.

1960s J. L. Carr, Kettering. Illustrated by J. L. Carr; undated. Pale brown and white covers, text on white paper. There was a later reprint in purple and white card covers, with text on pale blue paper; another in blue and mauve glazed card covers, with text on blue paper. Pp. 16. 12.5 × 92 cm.

1970 Heinemann, London. Illustrated by Helen Oxenbury; in colour and monochrome. Pictorial paperboards, in green, lettered in white and turquoise, with the picture from p. 29 in a circle, with added colour and background. The back cover has the Jubjub from p. 33, again in full colour. Marching dust jacket; back flap has a photograph of Oxenbury and reviews. Issued at 22s. (£1.10). Pp. 48. 27.8 × 21.3 cm.

Published in the same year in New York by Franklin Watts, in identical format at $4.95.

Reissued in 1983 in laminated pictorial boards as the first-edition cover.

1973 Simon & Schuster, New York. *The Snark Puzzle Book* by Martin Gardner. Yellow cloth boards, with bird (from the back cover of the first edition, but in reverse) in black on the upper front cover; title in black on the spine. Pale green dust jacket, with title based on the Holiday bell-buoy design, on a turquoise background; title on the spine in brown, green, and black. Includes all the Holiday pictures and seventy-five "Snark-teasers", with answers proved in the appendix. "*Jabberwocky*" also included with the Tenniel pictures. Pp. 138 (last two leaves blank). 23.6 × 16.7 cm. Price $5.95.

1973 Normal, Illinois. Illustrations by Arlene Bennett. Twenty-six unnumbered pages of hand-lettered text with fourteen pictures ranging from tiny marginalia to half-page illustrations. Limited edition of sixty-five numbered copies, signed by the illustrator; hand bound under the guidance of Oliver Fancher at Illinois State University.

1974 Catalpa Press, London. Illustrations by Byron Sewell, introduction by Martin Gardner. Black cloth boards, with pocket inside back cover enclosing cards with sections of the crew members' faces, so that they can be resorted. A limited issue of 250 numbered copies signed by the illustrator. A highly elaborate version; a section of the sheets is given over to a picture of the vessel and crew in a single concertinaed sheet. There are other special effects, which altogether make a page count misleading, if not impossible. 30.2 × 21 cm. Issued at £25. A single-leaf prospectus was issued; 20.8 × 14.8 cm.

1975 The Whittington Press, Andoversford. Line illustrations by Harold Jones. A limited edition of 750 numbered copies signed by the illustrator, including thirty bound in full leather. Black cloth boards (or leather) with title in gilt on the front cover within an ornamental frame; title, publisher's mascot, and four sets of double lines in gilt on the spine. Top edge gilt; others uncut, a fine and luxurious production. Pp. 48. 29 × 19 cm. Issued at £15 (£30 for the leather copies).

1975 Michael Dempsey, London. Monochrome illustrations by Ralph Steadman. Plain beige cloth boards; title in black on the spine. Yellow dust jacket with title in illustrator's script with the picture from p. 37. Pp. 72. 27.9 × 26 cm. Issued at £4.50. One hundred fifty copies included an etching, numbered and signed by the artist.

Six of the pictures were issued, in sixty-five numbered sets, in a portfolio of etchings printed by Cliff White of White Ink Limited, signed and titled by the artist, at £150. The book was published in New York by Clarkson Potter in 1976, in grey paper jackets; front cover has the picture from p. 37 with title, etc., in black and white; back cover has account of the book, author, and illustrator. 27.5 × 25.7 cm.

1976 John Minnion, London. Line illustrations by John Minnion. Blue paper jackets. The front cover has, in black, the title and an extra picture, the back cover another extra picture, with short biographical note. Pictures on every page interwoven with text in the illustrator's own script. A personal tour de force. Pp. 39. 29.5 × 21 cm. Issued at £1.50.

1976 Folio Society, London. Illustrations by Quentin Blake. Cloth boards, with an extra colour picture of the chase extending over both covers. Title in gilt on the spine. Text set in Bell type, appropriately. Issued in a pale blue paperboards slipcase. Available to members of the society at £3.95. Pp. 52. 22.1 × 15.5 cm.

1980 Windward (W. H. Smith), Leicester. A facsimile of the 1876 first edition. Cream paperboards, with first-edition cover designs in black; the spine has the publisher and title in roman uppercase reading upward, black endpapers. Pale brown dust jacket with matching designs in dark brown. The spine has the title reading downward; the front flap has text about the volume, the back flap a brief Carroll biography. Issued at £2.95. Pp. xiv, 83. 18.6 × 12.3 cm.

American issue published by Mayflower Books, New York, identical to the above, apart from the publisher on the title page and wording on the title page reverse, and change of publisher on the dust jacket and spine. Issued at $7.95.

1981 Barbara J. Raheb, Tarzana, California. One unsigned illustration. Edition limited to three hundred copies, signed by the publisher. Blue paperboards lettered and decorated in gilt. Miniature edition. 2.2 × 1.5 cm.

1981 William Kaufmann, Inc., in cooperation with Bryn Mawr College Library, Los Altos, California. Lewis Carroll's "The Hunting of the Snark," illustrated by Henry Holiday. Centennial edition, edited by James Tanis and John Dooley. This fine volume, printed by the Stinehour Press, includes a complete facsimile of the first edition, followed by the full text again—with annotations by Martin Gardner, an essay "The Designs for the Snark" by Charles Mitchell, a suite of plates of Holiday's drawings and related topics, and "The Listing of the Snark" by Selwyn Goodacre. It was issued in several formats:

    a. Subscriber's edition—limited to 395 numbered copies, signed by the participants. Quarter leather, cloth board covers, with separate suite of the plates, all within publisher's box.

    b. Collector's edition—limited to 1,995 copies. Red cloth boards, title, etc., on spine on black stick-on label.

    c. Trade edition—5,000 copies. Black cloth boards, lettered in red, in red dust jacket. Lettered in black and white with Holiday picture on the front. "Reprinted with emendations in February 1982."

    d. The section "The Listing of the Snark" issued as a separate offprint of fifty-seven copies for Selwyn Goodacre.

1983 University of California Press, Berkeley. Illustrated by Barry Moser and with an Introduction by James R. Kincaid. Blue paper jackets, with embossed title. Pp. 44. 34 × 21.3 cm. First trade edition. Also issued as:

    a. Edition limited to one hundred copies numbered and signed by Moser, with five of the printed illustrations, signed by Moser, loosely inserted.

b. Published by the University of California Press for the Lewis Carroll Society of North America as Carroll Studies Number 7 in a limited edition of 350, signed by Moser.

1989 Carroll Foundation, Flemington, Australia. Illustrated by Frank Hinder, with an introductory essay by John Pauli and explanatory poems by Hinder. Black paperboards, with design and title, etc., on front cover and spine in gilt. Pp. 64. 24.6 × 19 cm. Also issued as a limited edition of one hundred copies signed and numbered by the illustrator, in white cloth boards.

1992 Lewis Carroll Society of North America, New York. Illustrated by Jonathan Dixon. First edition limited to 450 copies. Black cloth with pictures and title, etc., in silver. Also issued in a deluxe edition limited to fifty copies, each with an extra sketch. Bound as the standard edition but with pictures and title, etc., in gilt. A number of hand-coloured prints from the book were also issued. Pp. 90. 27.9 × 21.2 cm.

1993 Macmillan, London. With an introduction by Selwyn Goodacre. The only edition to be printed, by the original publishers, from the original wood blocks. This was done by Ian Mortimer at his Press, I. M. Imprint, London. 25.9 × 18.2 cm. It was issued in several formats:
a. Numbers 1–55 bound in full leather and presented in a slipcase with a portfolio of separate prints of the nine woodengravings.
b. Numbers 56–130 quarter bound in cloth over paperboards and presented in a slipcase with the prints.
c. Numbers 131–430 quarter bound in cloth over paperboards in a slipcase.
A trade edition was issued, without the Goodacre introduction. "A faithful photographic reproduction of the poem and its illustrations in the limited edition."

1994 Tome Press, Missouri. Illustrations by Henry Holiday. Paperback. Pp. 32. 25.6 × 92 cm.

1995 Privately printed by Gavin O'Keefe, Victoria, Australia. Illustrated by Gavin O'Keefe. Red paper jackets, with paste-on white label with picture, title, etc., in black. Pp. 41. 21.1 × 14.7 cm.

1997 Angerona Press, Ryde, Isle of Wight. *The Hunting of the Snark Concluded,* by Cathy Bowern, illustrations by Brian Puttock. The book starts with the full text of the *Snark,* with Puttock illustrations. This is followed by Bowern's sequel, also illustrated by Puttock. Cream cloth boards, lettered on spine in gilt. Full-colour dust jacket. Pp. 121. 21 × 14.7 cm.

1997 Angerona Press, Ryde, Isle of Wight. *The Snark Decoded* by Cathy Bowern, illustrations by Brian Puttock. The full text of the *Snark,* and the sequel, are reprinted, now with full notes by Bowen on both. Paperback. Pp. 142. 21 × 14.7 cm.

2000 Privately printed, St. Petersburg. Text is hand written by Yuri Shtapakov and surrounded by hand-coloured drypoint engravings. Quarto portfolio. Pp. 49. Housed in original folding case of multicolored leather onlays, with an inset featuring one of the engravings on each panel. A personal tour de force. Only two copies produced.

2010 Evertype, Westport, Ireland. *The Hunting of the Snark: An Agony in Eight Fits.* Illustrated by Henry Holiday. A standard edition typeset with Evertype's *Annotated-Alice*-inspired Carrollian typography. ISBN 978-1-904808-36-7.

2010 Melville House, Brooklyn. *The Hunting of the Snark: An Agony in Eight Fits.* Illustrated and with an illustrator's note by Mahendra Singh. ISBN 978-1-935554-24-0

2011 Studio Treasure, Toronto. *The Hunting of the Snark: An Agony in Eight Fits.* Illustrations and design by Oleg Lipchenko. Limited edition of 100 signed and numbered copies. ISBN 978-0-9783613-2-7

2016 Macmillan Children's Books, London. Illustrated by Chris Riddell. ISBN 978-1-5098-1433-6

2018 Cheshire Cat Press, Toronto. *The Hunting of the Snark: An Agony in Eight Fits.* With twelve illustrations by Byron W. Sewell and an Introduction by Edward Wakeling. Illustrator's note by Byron W. Sewell. Hand printed in a limited edition of 42 signed and numbered copies.

2019 Chevington Press, Goole. *The Hunting of the Snark, An Agony in Eight Fits.* Illustrated by D. R. Wakefield, and etched paper covers. Quarter light brown morocco with 13 etchings, etched nameplates, and etched paper covers. Limited edition of 23 copies. 38 × 29 cm.

2022 The Reading Room Press, Quenington. *The Hunting of the Snark.* Illustrated by Ian Corfe-Stephens. Limited to 63 copies. 28 cm.

TRANSLATIONS

The countries are listed chronologically, in order of their first *Snark* translations.

FRENCH

1929 *La Chasse au Snark,* **Hours Press** (Nancy Cunard), Chapelle-Reanville-Eure. Translated by Louis Aragon, unillustrated. A limited edition of ten copies on Japon, numbered from 1 to 5, with five not for sale; and 350 copies on Alfa, numbered from 1 to 300, with fifty not for sale. Each copy signed by the translator. Red paperboards with title, etc., in both languages on the front cover in black. Pp. 38. 23 × 22 cm.
Reprinted by P. Seghers, Paris, in 1949. White jackets, pp. 45, 18 × 11 cm, no illustrations. Reprinted again in 1962. Stiff jackets, with a picture on the front cover in green and purple by Mario Prassinos, pp. 69, 16 × 13.3 cm. Also reprinted in 1959 in red cloth and in November 1980 as a paperback, with front cover picture by Patrick Vanhoutte.

1940 *La Chasse au Snark,* **Librairie José Corti, Paris.** Translated by Henri Parisot, unillustrated. A limited edition of 255 unnumbered copies, 5 on Madagascar and 250 on Alfa. Stiff white card jackets, with title, etc., on the front cover in black. Pp. 32 (iii) . 24.5 × 15.5 cm.

1945 *La Chasse au Snark, de suivide fantasmagorie et de Poeta Fit, Non Nascitur,* **Seghers, Paris.** Translated by Henri Parisot. Also includes "Fantasmagorie" and "Poeta Fit, Non Nascitur". White card jackets, with title in red, the rest in black. Pp. 108, (iv). 19 × 14.3 cm. Edges uncut. Limited edition of sixty numbered copies on Fil Johannot, 2,000 on velin, some H.C.

1946 *La Chasse au Snark et Autres Poèmes*, **Fontaine, Paris.** Translated by Henri Parisot ("revue et corrigée"), illustrations by Gisele Prassinos. The additional poems are the two directly above, plus "Le Morse et le Charpentier, Assis sur une Barrière et Jabberwocky". White card jackets, title, etc., in black, intertwining picture of the Snark (?) in green and red. Pp. 140 (plus one leaf) numbered from front cover. Limited edition of 7 numbered copies on vergé de Hollande, with "un dessin original de Gisele Prassinos", 25 on marais crèvecœur, 1,500 on velin, plus some H.C.

1948 *La Chasse au Snark*, **G. L. M., Paris.** Translated by Florence Gilliam and Guy Levis Mano, illustrated by Henry Holiday. A limited edition of 1,080 copies, and 25 for *"les amis de G. L. M."* Includes the English text. There was a new edition in 1970, published by Le Club Français du Livre (pp. 146) and a further edition in 1980.

1950 *La Chasse au Snark*, **Éditions Premières, Paris.** A new translation by Henri Parisot, illustrations by Max Ernst. In the series L'Age d'Or. Issued in a limited edition of 775 numbered copies, numbers 1–25 on marais crèvecœur, with a signed and numbered colour etching and an embossed design inscribed "Carte de l'océan" by Ernst, and numbers 26–775 on Alfama (there were a few copies "hors commerce"). Pp. 72. 16.7 × 13.2 cm.

1952 *Lewis Carroll, une Étude*, **P. Seghers, Paris.** A translation by Henri Parisot is included in his biography of Lewis Carroll (in the series Poètes d'aujourd'hui). One of the Ernst illustrations is included.

1962 *La Chasse au Snark*, **Jean-Jacques Pauvert, France.** Translated by Henri Parisot, illustrations by Henry Holiday. A limited edition of 1,999 numbered copies, 1–30 on pur du marais, 31–1,999 on offset alfa bellegarde. Blue paper jackets with the title, etc., in black on the front with a reproduction in the center of the first-edition cover—front and back on the front and back, in black and white. Pp. ix, 82. 18.2 × 13 cm.

1969 *Le Rire des Poètes*, **Pierre Belfond, Paris.** Translated by Henri Parisot. Pp. 26–76 are a selection of Carroll verses, including the *Snark*.

1971 *Through the Looking-Glass and The Hunting of the Snark*, **Aubier-Flammarion, Paris.** Translated by Henri Parisot, the *Snark* is on pp. 248–299. It is followed by a suite of illustrations by Max Ernst. The text in English is on the left-hand page, the French on the right. Stiff paper jackets. The front cover has the title, etc., in brown and black, with a photograph of Dodgson below on the right, with a brown rectangle on the left. The back cover has the opening paragraph from *Looking-Glass* (bilingual) with the Dodgson photograph above. Pp. 318. 17.8 × 10.9 cm.

Reprinted in 1976, with an extended list of books at the end "dans la même collection". Red stiff paper jackets, with title, etc., in back and white and with a "butterfly blot" picture. On the back in white is "Lewis Carroll" and "en bilingue". The *Snark* is revised again.

In a letter to the present writer, M. Parisot stated that he first translated the *Snark* in 1940, and subsequently reworked it about ten times, before producing his definitive version for the Aubier-Flammarion bilingual edition in 1976.

1981 *La Chasse au Snark*, **Garance, Paris and Geneva.** Text français de Jacques Roubard, mise en image(s) de Annie-Claude Martin. Thirty-two separate sheets, printed on one side only; in printed red board case, with picture on the front cover. 32 × 25 cm.

1986 *Tout Alice et La Chasse au Snark*, **Éditions Aubier Montaigne, France.** Translated by Henri Parisot, illustrated by Ralph Steadman.

1996 *La Chasse au Snark*, **Éditions Mille et Une Nuits, France.** Translated by Bernard Hoepffner. Pp. 64. 15.5 × 10.5 cm.

1997 *La Chasse au Snark*, **Collection Théâtre d'Expressions, France.** Translated by Fabrice Eberhard, illustrated by Gregory Lhomme. Text in French and English. Paperback, pp. 114. 20 × 11.8 cm.

1998 *La Chasse au Snark*, **Bubble Gum News, France.** Translated by François Naudin. Card covers over loose sheets with spine binder. Pp. 20. 29.6 × 21.1 cm.

1999 *La Chasse au Snark*, **La Double vue La Différence, Paris.** Illustrated by Julio Pomar, translated by Gerard Gacon, with essays by

Gerard Gacon and Gerard-Georges Lemaire. Glazed paperboards with colour pictures on front and back. Pp. 120. 23.7 × 29.5 cm.

LATIN

1934 *The Hunting of the Snark*, **Macmillan, London.** Rendered into Latin verse, in Virgilian hexameters, by Percival Robert Brinton, D.D. (Rector of Hambledon, Buckinghamshire). Unillustrated. English text is on the left-hand page, Latin on the right. Red paper jackets, lettered in gilt, black blank. Pp. vi, 58. 19.3 × 13 cm.

1936 *The Hunting of the Snark*, **Shakespeare Head Press, sold by Basil Blackwell, Oxford.** Translated into Latin elegiacs by H. D. Watson, with a foreword by Gilbert Murray. Unillustrated. English text is on the left-hand page, Latin on the right. Dark blue cloth boards, title, etc., on the front in gilt and on the spine. All edges uncut. The translation was directly inspired by the 1934 Brinton translation (above). The volume includes several other poems by the translator, along with their Latin translations. Pp. xvi, 116. 19 × 12.8 cm.

ITALIAN

1945 *La Caccia allo Snarco*, **Magi-Spinette, Rome.** Translated by Cesare Vico Lodovici. Illustrations by Ketty Castellucci. Pp. 79.

1985 *La caccia allo Squado*, **Studio Tesi, Italy.** Translated by Milli Griffi.

1989 *La Caccia allo Snark*, **S. E., Milan.** Translated and with an afterword by Roberto Sanesi. A bilingual edition, with the Holiday illustrations.

SWEDISH

1959 *Snarkjakten*, **Holger Schildts Förlag, Helsingfors.** Translated by Lars Forssell. Illustrations by Tove Jansson in line from pen-and-ink drawings. Stiff paper jackets, the front cover off white with a picture in green, black, and blue; title, etc., in black, and also on the spine. The back cover has a drawing from the text. Pp. 56. 22 × 14.2 cm. Issued at 9.75 Kr.

Danish

1963 *Snarkejagten*, Det Schonbergske Forlag, Copenhagen. Translated by Christopher Maaløe. English text on the left, Danish on the right. Paper jackets; the front cover has a photographic reproduction of a fabric picture of a Snark with a bathing-machine sporting Union Jack wheels. Pp. 77. 22.3 × 15.7 cm.

German

1968 *Die Jagd nach dem Schnark*, Insel Verlag, Frankfurt am Main. Translated by Klaus Reichert. English text on the left-hand page, German on the right. Illustrations by Henry Holiday. Paperboards, the covers designed in the style of the first edition, but in purple on green, and with the addition of a paper label with the title, etc., and a similar label on the spine. The volume matches the edition of *Alice's Adventures in Wonderland* and *Letters to Child Friends*, all three volumes are in the series Insel-Bucherei. The *Snark* is "Nr. 934". Pp. 96. 18 × 11.6 cm.
New edition 1982, entirely reset, pale mauve paper jackets. Front cover has the Bellman's uncle picture, with title, etc., all in black. Pp. 119. 17.6 × 10.7 cm.

1988 *Die Jagd nach dem Schnark*, Edition Weitbrecht, Stuttgart. An edition to accompany the musical version (see below). Includes the libretto, plus the full English text of the *Snark*. Pp. 143.

1996 *Die Jagd nach dem Schnark*, Philipp Reclam jun., Stuttgart. English and German edition. Translated by Oliver Sturm. Orange paper jackets, with cover illustrations of the Banker's fate without the Bellman. Pp. 98. 14.8 × 9.7 cm.

Spanish

1970 *La Caza del Snark*, Calatayud-Dea, Buenos Aires. Apparently a second edition. No details available of first publication, but the volume is illustrated. Pp. 75.

1971 *Le Caza del Snark.* Translated by Ulalume González de León. In *Plural*, no. 2, November 1971.

1980 *El Riesgo del Placer*, **Biblioteca Era Poesía, Mexico.** Includes *La Caza del Snark*, translated by Ulalume González de León.

1982 *La Caza del Snark*, **Ediciones Libertarias.** Translated by Leopoldo María Panero, illustrated by Henry Holiday and Jesús Gabán.

1982 *La Caza del Snark*, **Ediciones Mascarón.** Translated by María Eugenia Frutos and J. J. Laborda, illustrated by Henry Holiday.

1986 *Alicia en el país de las maravillas, Alicia a través del espejo, La Caza del Snark*, **Plaza y Janes Editores.** Translated and with an introduction by Luis Maristany.

2022 *La Caza del Snark.* **Alfaguara Infantil, Mexico.** Translated and illustrated by Juan Gedovius. ISBN 978-607-381212-2

JAPANESE

1972 Book of Modern Poetry Vol. 2: Lewis Carroll, Shicho-sha, Tokyo. A translation by 沢崎順之助 (Sawazaki Junnosuke). The *Snark* is included on pp. 264–303.

1977 『ルイス・キャロル詩集 －不思議の国の言葉たち』 *Poems of Lewis Carroll*, 筑摩書房 **(Chikuma Shobo), Tokyo.** Includes a translation of the Snark by 高橋康也 (Takahashi Yasunari) and 沢崎順之助 (Sawazaki Junnosuke). Reprinted in a pocket-size edition in 1989.

Yoshiyuka Momma tells me of three Japanese books with Snark titles which in fact are not translations but are works inspired by the *Snark*.

POLISH

1973 Literatura na Świecie, no. 5. Includes a translation: *Wyprawa na żmirłacza. Męka w ośmiu konwulsjach* 'Expedition to hunt the snark. A torment in eight convulsions' by Robert Stiller.

DUTCH

1977 *De Jacht op de Trek*, Uitgeverij J. Couvreur, The Hague. Translated by Erdwin Spits. Illustrations by Inge Vogel. Stiff paper jackets in metallic green, with title, etc., and pictures in maroon. The front cover has the ship approaching with a large bird in the foreground; the back cover has the ship sailing away. Pp. 44. 19.3 × 3 cm.

1977 *De Jacht op de Strok*, Drukwerk, Amsterdam. Translated by Evert Geradts and with his own illustrations. Paperboards; the covers have a close design of green leaves on a yellow background, title in green in a white background; above is a circular paste-on picture of forks and "Hope" (represented as the upper half of a nude female figure); the back cover has a triangular paste-on picture, again of "Hope", but with thimbles. Issued in a cellophane dust jacket lettered in black, with author and translator, etc. The book ends with an eight-page "Nawoord" by Geradts, with a photograph. Pp. 104. 22.1 × 13.8 cm.

1987 *The Hunting of the Snark (A Delirium in Eight Crises)*, Dedalus, Antwerpen. Van Paul Pourveur naar Lewis Carroll: 1987. Paperback. Dramatized version. Accompanied by a 33-rpm LP record, with record sleeve and one sheet insert. All in a grey card box, decorated with Carroll's drawing of himself lecturing (with hand over mouth).

2001 *De Jacht op de Snark*, Hassink Drukkers, Haaksbergen. Translated and with annotations by Henri Riuzenaar, illustrated by Iris Cousijnsen. Blue paperboards, lettered in white, with full-colour picture from the book. Back cover has a picture of Riuzenaar. Text includes English text. Limited to two hundred copies, in matching slipcase. 23 × 29 cm.

RUSSIAN

1982 *Охота на Змеря (Okhota na Zmeria)*. Translated by Vladimir Orël. In the journal *Иностранная литература (Inostrannaia literatura)*, no. 10; 231–4.

1991 *Охота на Снарка: Агония в восьми воплах (Okhota na Snarka: Agoniia v vos'mi voplakh)*, Rukitis, Moscow. Translated by Grigorii Kruzhkov, illustrated by Leonid Tishkov. Grey decorated paperboards.

Pp. 88. 24 × 15.5 cm. There is a variant issue in white decorated paperboards.

1993 *Охота на Снарка: химера о восьми главах* (*Okhota na Snarka: khimera o vos'mi glavakh*), Krug, Moscow. Translated by I. Lipkin, illustrated by L. Zalesskii. Blue paper jackets.

1999 *Охота на Снарка: Переполох в восьми охах* (*Okhota na Snarka: Perepolokh v vos'mi okhakh*), Eksmo Press, Moscow. Translated by Leonid Iakhnin and Iuli Dumilov, introduction by Leonid Iakhnin. Also includes the Alice books and *Letters to Children*. Pp. 606. 20 × 12.5 cm.

2016 *Охота на Снарка в Восьми Напастях* (*Okhota na Snarka v Vos'mi Napastiakh*): *The Hunting of the Snark in Russian*. Portlaoise, Evertype. Ed. Victor Fet. ISBN 978-1-78201-121-7.

HEBREW

1989 ציד הסנרק (*Tseid haSnarq*) ספריית מעריב - שבא הוצאת (Shva Publishers - Maariv Library), Israel. Translated by ניצה בן־ארי (Nitsa Ben-Ari), illustrated by דני קרמן (Danny Kerman).

2000 ת'סנרק מחפשים (*Mekhapsim taSnarq*) עכשיו ספרות (Sifrut Akhshav), Israel. Translated by יוני להב (Yoni Lahav), illustrated by אמי רוביגנר (Ami Rubinger).

BULGARIAN

1993 *Избрани произведения* (*Izbrani proizvedeniia*) Khipopo, Varna. Paperback. In three parts (Part 1: *Алиса в страната на чудесата* (*Alisa v stranata na chudesata*); Part 2: *Алиса в огледалния свят* (*Alisa v ogledalniia sviat*); Part 3: Phantasmagorias). The *Snark* is on pp. 29–51. Also includes other nonsense verse and *A Tangled Tale*.

FAROESE

1994 *Eftir Snarki*, Forlagið Sprotin. Illustrated by Axel Tórgarð. Glazed card jackets, with full-colour picture on front cover, author and blurb on the back. English text included. Pp. 80. 24 × 17 cm.

BELARUSIAN

(In press) *Снаркаловы: Прападаньне ў васьмі выкліках* (*Snarkalovy: Prapadan'ne ŭ vas'mi vyklikakh*). Translated by Max Ščur. Evertype, Dundee. ISBN 978-1-78201-158-3.

ARMENIAN

(In press) *Սնարքի Որսը: Հերոսապատում՝ ութ դրվագով* (*Snark'i Vorsy: Herosapatum` ut' drvagov*). Translated by Alexander Kalantaryan and Artak Kalantaryan. Evertype, Dundee. ISBN 978-1-78201-331-0.

ANTHOLOGIES INCLUDING
THE ENTIRE SNARK

Although I hope most examples are included, I cannot claim that this section is comprehensive. Certain volumes which properly belong here have been listed or mentioned earlier: *Rhyme? And Reason?* because of its importance in the narrative of the early history; the Parisot French translations, for the sake of clarity and continuity; and a number because they present the *Snark* as the main feature of the book—1899 Burt, 1903 Newell, 1939 Chameleon, and the 1936 Watson Latin translation. For the sake of clarity, where translations occur in anthologies, they are included in the relevant translations section.

The books listed here are cited only in their first editions and are listed in chronological order, with the year given fronted in each entry for ease of reading.

1902 *Nonsense Anthology*, collected by Carolyn Wells. Charles Scribner's Sons, New York. Includes "The Hunting of the Snark" (extract).

1924 *Alice's Adventures in Wonderland, Through the Looking-Glass and the Hunting of the Snark*, introduction by Alexander Woollcott. Modern Library, Boni & Liveright, New York.

1929 *Alice in Wonderland, Through the Looking-Glass and Other Comic Pieces*, Everyman's Library. Dent/Dutton, London/New York.

—— *The Collected Verse of Lewis Carroll*. E. P. Dutton & Co., New York.

1930 *Alice in Wonderland with The Hunting of the Snark, and Poems from Sylvie and Bruno*, ed. Guy N. Pocock. King's Treasuries of Literature. J. M. Dent, London.

1931 *The Lewis Carroll Book*, ed. Richard Herrick. Dial Press, New York.

1932 *Alice's Adventures in Wonderland, Through the Looking-Glass and The Hunting of the Snark*, introduction by Mrs. F. D. Roosevelt. Jacket Library, National House Library Foundation, Washington, D.C.

—— *The Collected Verse of Lewis Carroll*. Macmillan, London.

1933 *The Collected Verse of Lewis Carroll*. The Macmillan Co., New York.

1934 *Logical Nonsense: The Works of Lewis Carroll*, eds. Philip C. Blackburn and Lionel White. G. P. Putnam's Sons, New York.

1936 *Nonsensibus …*, by D. B. Wyndham Lewis. Methuen, London.

—— *The Complete Works of Lewis Carroll*, introduction by Alexander Woollcott. Random House, New York.

1939 *Poems Selected from the Works of Lewis Carroll*. Macmillan, London.

c.1930s *Alice's Adventures in Wonderland, Through the Looking-Glass and The Hunting of the Snark*. Carlton House, New York.

c.1940s *Alice's Adventures in Wonderland, Through the Looking-Glass and The Hunting of the Snark, with illustrations by John Tenniel*. Blue Ribbon Books, New York.

1950 *Poets of the English Language, vol. 5, Tennyson to Yeats*, eds. W. H. Auden and Norman Holmes Pearson. Viking Press, London.

—— *The Humorous Verse of Lewis Carroll*, ed. J. E. Morpurgo. Grey Walls Press, London. In the Crown Classics series.

1951 *Lewis Carroll's Alice in Wonderland and Other Favourites*. Pocket Books, New York.

1954 *Alice's Adventures in Wonderland, Through the Looking-Glass and other Writings*, introduction by Robin Deniston. Collins, London and Glasgow.

1956. *The Book of Nonsense by Many Authors*, ed. Roger Lancelyn Green. Dent, London. In the Children's Illustrated Classics series.

1957 *The Silver Treasury of Light Verse*, ed. Oscar Williams. New American Library, New York. A Mentor Book.

1959 *Lewis Carroll, Nonsense Verse*. Edward Hulton, London. In the Pocket Poets series.

1960 *The Sapphire Treasury of Stories for Boys and Girls*, ed. Gillian Avery. Gollanz, London.

1961 *The World of Victorian Humor*, ed. Harold Orel. Appleton-Century-Crofts, New York.

1963 *Alice's Adventures in Wonderland, Through the Looking-Glass, and The Hunting of the Snark.* Nonesuch Press, London. Published under the Bodley Head imprint in 1974. A Nonesuch Cygnet.

1964 *The Oxford Book of Nineteenth Century Verse,* ed. John Hayward. Oxford University Press, London.

1965 *The Works of Lewis Carroll,* ed. Roger Lancelyn Green. Spring Books, Paul Hamlyn, London.

1971 *Alice in Wonderland,* ed. Donald J Grey. W. W. Norton, New York. A Norton Critical Edition.

1973 *Poems of Lewis Carroll,* selected by Myra Cohn Livingston. Thomas Y. Crowell, New York.

1978 *The Illustrated Lewis Carroll,* ed. Roy Gasson. Jupiter Books, London.

1979 *The Faber Book of Nonsense Verse,* ed. Geoffrey Grigson. Faber, London.

1982 *The Complete Illustrated Works of Lewis Carroll,* ed. E. Guiliano. Avenel Books, New York.

—— *The Complete Illustrated Works of Lewis Carroll.* Chancellor Press, London.

1983 *The Oxford Book of Narrative Verse,* chosen and edited by Iona and Peter Opie. Oxford University Press, Oxford and New York.

1986 *The Complete Alice & The Hunting of the Snark,* illustrated by Ralph Steadman. Jonathan Cape, London.

c.1992 *The Best of Lewis Carroll, illustrated by John Tenniel and Henry Holiday.* Castle, New York.

1998 *Utter Nonsense, illustrated by Henry Holiday and Harry Furniss.* Folio Society, London.

2001 *The Complete Stories and Poems of Lewis Carroll.* First published in 2001 by Geddes & Grosset, an imprint of Children's Leisure Products Limited, for Midpoint Press, New Lanark, Scotland.

2006. *The Annotated Hunting of the Snark: The Definitive Edition.* Edited with a preface and notes by Martin Gardner. Introduction by Adam Gopnik. Original illustrations by Henry Holiday. W. W. Norton: New Yor and London. ISBN 978-0-393-06242-7.

THEATRICAL AND MUSICAL ADAPTATIONS, AND RECORDINGS

I am indebted to Charles Lovett's book *Alice on Stage* (Meckler, Westport, Conn., 1990) for details of many of the following productions.

1960 A reading by Boris Karloff, Caedmon Records. Includes "The Pied Piper".

1963 A reading by Alec Guinness on BBC radio on 24 December 1963. Alan Tannenbaum has a copy of the 34-page script.

c1970 Adapted by Anthony Gash, presented at Magdalen College, Oxford University.

1971 Operatic version by Bill Tchakirides, presented by Systems Theater at the Whitney Museum, New York, September 1971.

1978 Operatic version presented by the Queens College Departments of Music and Drama and Theatre at the Queens College Theatre, Queens, New York, 13–16 April 1978.

1980 A French version by Ludovic Flament was presented (no further details to hand).

1982 A French version by Jean-Marie Boyer, with music by Denis Lefebvre du Prey, was presented at the Théâtre Atelier du Luxembourg, Paris, as part of the Festival Foire Saint-Germain, 11 June–2 July 1982.

—— Version presented by June Alleyn's School in London, 8–9 July 1982. An operetta with music specially written for the production with some traditional tunes added.

—— *The Hunting of the Snark*, music by Douglas Young. Cameo Classics, Manchester, England. LP record.

1984 Version by R. E. Jackson, with music by David Ellis, presented by the Children's Musical Theatre of Mobile, Alabama, as a touring production.

c.1986 Portuguese production in Lisbon.

1987 Mike Batt's *The Hunting of the Snark* was first performed at the Royal Albert Hall in London on Wednesday, 1 April 1987. A subsequent full dramatization was produced on the London stage a year later and closed after only a few performances. An earlier LP record version was also issued.

—— *Lewis Carroll's The Hunting of the Snark*, a Musical Comedy, by R. Eugene Jackson, music by David Ellis: I. E. Clark, Inc., Schulenburg, Texas. Grey paper jackets, spine and lettering in orange.

1988 German version by Michael Ende, music by Wilfried Hiller, performed at the Staatstheater am Gartnerplatz, Munich, 16 January 1988.

1992 *Hunting of the Snark*, a musical interpretation by Anne Nordheim for trombone, organ, and electronic music: Euridice, Oslo. Recorded at a live concert in September 1991.

1993 *Alice in Wonderland*, CD-ROM: Queue, Inc., and Clearvue, Inc., Fairfield, Conn. Includes the *Snark*.

1999 Set of audio cassettes of works by Lewis Carroll, with extra notes. Includes the *Snark*. Entertainment Software, Inc., Commuter's Library, Ardington, Texas.

2000 Crazy Horse Theatre Company presented a dramatic version at the Museum of Oxo Tower Wharf, South Bank, London, 11–29 April 2000.

2002 *Jabberwocky, Stuff and Nonsense*, read by Griffin Rogers and Brianna Voss: Painted Wings Film, audio CD, with pictorial insert. Includes the *Snark*, read by Rogers.

Undated. French version presented at Théâtre de Plaisance, Paris.

Undated. Play based on the Alice books and the *Snark* at Belmont Elementary School (precise location unknown).

CANDLE-ENDS

1936 *A Rime of Three Worthies*, by Ashley Ohmsted: privately printed, Edgartown, Mass. A limited edition of ten numbered copies, composed at the office of the *Vineyard Gazette* and imprinted in the shop of the Martha's Vineyard Printing Co., Oak Bluffs, Mass. Green half-cloth, decorated paperboards in green and beige on cream. This curiosity is a full-length parody of the *Snark*. It falls well short of the original. Pp. 22 plus four blank leaves at the beginning and three at the end. 23.9 × 15.5 cm.

1941 *The Snark Was a Boojum*, by Richard Shattuck (pseudonym of Dora Richards Shattuck): William Morrow, New York; Robert Hale, London. A mystery novel, each chapter beginning with four lines from the Snark.

1973 Complete manuscript of the *Snark*, transcribed and illustrated by Charles E. Wright. Unpublished—in the Edward Wakeling collection. Separate sheets, 35.3 × 27.8 cm. The transcription, in a fine personalized script, covers forty sheets, preceded by the title sheet, and a suite of fourteen sheets, each with one of the thirteen characters and the author. A fine production that one might think merits publication.

1975 The Caxton Club of Chicago issued a "keepsake" on the occasion of its meeting on 19 November 1975. Reproduces the map and three stanzas. Printed by David Woodward, designed by R. Hunter Middleton, and signed by both.

1976 *Fit for a Beaver: "Fit the First" from THE HUNTING OF THE SNARK*, by Lewis Carroll, illustrations by Byron W. Sewell, Chicken Little's Press, Austin, Texas. A limited edition of thirty numbered and signed copies. Tan paper jackets with title and picture on the front cover in black matching the title page. One picture per verse, quite different from the Sewell full-length version (1974) noted above under English-Language Editions. Printed on side of the leaf only. Twenty-seven leaves. 28 × 21.5 cm.

—— *The Hunting of the Snark, Fit the First*, by Lewis Carroll, illustrations by Byron W. Sewell, privately printed by Byron W. Sewell, Austin, Texas. A limited edition of eight numbered and signed copies. Black stiff card jackets, with title, etc., on the front in gilt. The text, printed from the illustrator's own script, is on one side of the leaf only, apart from the title page, which has the imprint and copyright notice on the reverse. Each obverse merits a leaf to itself. The verses are interspersed at intervals with the illustrations which are hand-pulled lithographs in colour on German etching paper. Each is mounted on grey card, protected by a tissue guard, and attached only at the top so that the title, limitation note, and signature in pencil can be read on the reverse. The pictures may be described as symbolic in style; the symbolism is more obscure in some than in others. Twenty-five leaves. 27.5 × 21.5 cm.

Byron W. Sewell continued to issue strange Snark items, many of them single sheets, in minute numbers in the years 2000 to 2004 (see below for his 2000 Millennium Snark Trilogy).

1983 *"Snark Island"* stamps. These are what are called, in the Philatelic world, "Cinderella stamps". Created by Gerald King. A priced catalogue, with an introduction by Selwyn Goodacre, was issued in May 1983.

1984 *The Hunting of the Snark—Fit the Ninth—the Homecoming*, written by Richard Garnett for the fiftieth anniversary of the Snark

Club at King's College Cambridge, Wednesday, 30 May 1984. Fifty copies printed by Simon Rendall. Pp. 4 folded card. 19 × 12.8 cm.

1991 *The Hunting of the Snark*, a children's World War II play, by Bob Hescott and Stephen Cockett: Collins Educational, London.

1992 *The Cooking of the Snark Act II*, The Snarks Ltd., New York.

1996 *The Hunting of the Snark, Second Expedition*, by Peter Wesley-Smith, illustrations by Paul Stanish: Cherry Books, Camperdown, Australia.

1998 *The Hunting of the Snark, Eighth Fit*, translated into French without using the letter *e*, "traduire La Contrainte, Formules No. 2": L'Age D'Homme.

—— *"The Booking"*—A Missing Fit from Lewis Carroll's *The Hunting of the Snark*, by Charlie Lovett: privately printed. Republished in 2012 in *The Haunting of the Snarkasbord* (see below).

2000 *The Hunting of the Snark*, program for the Lewis Carroll Society Christmas Party, December 2000. Includes an essay on the Snark by Selwyn Goodacre. Six-page stapled booklet.

—— *The Sorting of the Snark*, by Roger Scowen: TGB Productions, London. An alphabetical list of words in the *Snark*.

—— *"The Recrewting"* and *"The Sailing"*, two unpublished fits from Lewis Carroll's sequel to *The Hunting of the Snark*, by Charlie Lovett: privately printed. Republished in 2012 in *The Haunting of the Snarkasbord* (see below).

—— *Snarkmaster*, by Byron Sewell: Storkling Press, Dead Deer, Alberta, Canada. An edition of fifteen copies, signed by the author. Part 1 of the Millennium Snark Trilogy. Republished in 2012 as *Snarkmaster: A Destiny in Eight Fits* (see below).

—— *Atchafalaya Boojum*, by Byron W. Sewell: Thousand Oaks Press, Calgary, 2000. An edition of ten copies, signed by the author. Part 2 of the Millennium Snark Trilogy. Republished in 2014 in *In the Boojum Forest* (see below).

—— *Snark! A Murderous Agony in Eight Fits*, by Byron Sewell: Thousand Oaks Press, Calgary, 2000. An edition of ten copies, signed by the author. Part 3 of the Millennium Snark Trilogy. Republished in 2014 as *Murder by Boojum* (see below).

2002 *Alice & The Snark*, by Everett Bleiler: Snark's Cave, New York, 2002. A limited edition of thirty-five numbered copies. A book of essays mainly about the *Snark*. Pp. 80. 20.5 × 14.8 cm.

2003 *The Translating of the Snark*, by Selwyn Goodacre and Mark R. Richards: Aznet Publishing, London. An attempt to list all known translations of the *Snark*.

2004 *A Snark Selection*, illustrated by Gavin O'Keefe, with Snarkian chapters by Harry Stephen Keeler: Ramble House, Shreveport, La.

2005 *Square Snark*, words by Lewis Carroll, edited by Alan Tannenbaum: privately printed. The *Snark* "translated" into Lewis Carroll's nyctographic script.

2011 *The West Virginia Snark Hunting Society*, by Byron W. Sewell: An edition of fifteen copies, signed by the author. Hand bound with relish fork by Victoria Sewell. Force Five Press, Hurricane West Virginia. Republished in 2016 in *Close Encounters of the Snarkian Kind* (see below).

2012 *The Haunting of the Snarkasbord*. A Portmanteau inspired by Lewis Carroll's *The Hunting of the Snark*. By Alison Tannenbaum, Byron W. Sewell, Charlie Lovett, & August A. Imholtz Jr. Illustrated by Byron W. Sewell. Westport, Evertype. ISBN 978-1-904808-98-5

—— *Snarkmaster: A Destiny in Eight Fits*. A Tale inspired by Lewis Carroll's *The Hunting of the Snark*. Written and illlustrated by Byron W. Sewell. (Millennium Snark Trilogy; 1) Westport, Evertype. ISBN 978-1-78201-002-9.

2014 *The Kaiser A Snark and The Baker*. A Keepsake Prepared by August A Imholtz, Jr and Byron Sewell. TUSC Christ Church Oxford 24 January 2014.

—— *In the Boojum Forest*. A Portmanteau inspired by Lewis Carroll's *The Hunting of the Snark*. Written and illlustrated by Byron W. Sewell. (Millennium Snark Trilogy; 2) Westport, Evertype. ISBN 978-1-78201-078-4.

—— *Murder by Boojum: A Mystery in Eight Fits* inspired by Lewis Carroll's *The Hunting of the Snark*. Written and illlustrated by Byron W. Sewell. (Millennium Snark Trilogy; 3) Westport, Evertype. ISBN 978-1-78201-079-1

2016 *Close Encounters of the Snarkian Kind:* A Portmanteau inspired by Lewis Carroll's *The Hunting of the Snark*. Written and illlustrated by Byron W. Sewell. Portlaoise, Evertype. ISBN 978-1-78201-134-7.

—— *The Hunting of the Snark: Ɏ Ψʀᴗⱪɯ ꞃᴕ ɏ 𐐝ᴗᴗɟⱷ (Dh Hunting uv dh Snark)*. An edition printed in the Deseret Alphabet. Portlaoise, Evertype. ISBN 978-1-78201-153-8.

2024 *The Millennium Snark Trilogy: Snarkmaster, Atchafalaya Boojum, Murder by Boojum.* Written and illlustrated by Byron W. Sewell. Dundee, Evertype. ISBN 978-1-78201-329-7.

—— *The Hunting of the Snark: An edition printed in the Nyctographic Square Alphabet devised by Lewis Carroll.* Illustrated by Henry Holiday. Dundee, Evertype. ISBN 978-1-78201-330-3.

The Listing of the Snark
Facsimile of the 1974 edition

When Selwyn presented me with the text of this book I was delighted to see it: his observations on Carroll's texts are always interesting and provocative. When I realized that Selwyn had been working on this text for more than *fifty years*, I thought a celebration was in order, so I put together a revision of *The Listing of the Snark* to include some notable additions to Snark publications, including the delicious contributions to Snarkology made by Byron W. Sewell.

As I was finalizing the book for publication, a first edition of Selwyn's *Listing* which I had found in an online bookshop was delivered to me. I do not know how many of the 80 copies of that still exist, but it seemed to me that publishing it in facsimile would round off the book nicely and share something rare with readers of *Engaging the Snark*.

Michael Everson

THE LISTING OF THE SNARK

BY

SELWYN H. GOODACRE

—a listing of editions and issues of

Lewis Carroll's

The Hunting of the Snark

from its inspiration on July 18, 1874

to July 18, 1974

The Listing of the Snark, Snark Day 1974.

Cover.

MACMILLAN — STANDARD EDITIONS

THE First Edition — first published 29 March 1876 (Macmillan's record), Carroll's own copy dated 30 March 1876. He wrote in 80 presentation copies on 29 March. He himself thought it should be published on 1st. April — "Surely that is the fittest day for it to appear".

The book is fully described in 'The Lewis Carroll Handbook', but there are 11 errors in the collation. The first 8 refer to the title-page:

1. add comma after 'Agony'
2. add stop after 'Fits'
3. the title of the 'Alice' books should be in double inverted commas, not single
4. AND should be in the upper case, not lower
5. The comma after GLASS should be a stop
6. The comma after WONDERLAND, and stop after GLASS should be inside the inverted commas, not outside
7. the line-end-stroke after GLASS should be double, not single
8. 'The Right ...Reserved' should be in lower case italics, not roman
9. The M signature should be in square brackets
10. As has been pointed out several times, the sphere at the top of the buoy on the back cover bears the letters IT
11. The lettering on the spine also has stops before THE, and after SNARK

As stated, the basic binding is buff-coloured cloth, but there are a number of variant bindings — not all (though most) were for presentation purposes, as copies are known with no inscription. The following is a complete list of the known variants:—

vellum and gold	light blue and gold	scarlet and gold
light green and gold	dark blue and gold	unglazed red, and
dark green and gold	crimson and gold	black

The Parrish collection also records copies in red sand-grain, red callico, red fine-ribbed, white parchment; and copies with plain or yellow edges, and even one with an inverted head on the cover (or does this refer to 'Sylvie and Bruno'? The Weaver article is not clear). A presentation copy in blue and gold has been described, probably a trial issue, the front cover has the Bellman and sail only, the back cover the bell-buoy.

Copies of the first edition are known in a grey dust-wrapper, and it is possible that all copies originally had them. The front cover has a reproduction of the title-page (including the date), the spine has the title

The Listing of the Snark, 1974:1.

in upright capitals (not sloping as suggested in 'The House of Macmillan' by Charles Morgan), the back cover has the advertisements.

The reprint dates are shown in later copies on the reverse of the title-page. It is very difficult to correlate these with the stated number of the 'thousand' that is found on the title-page in early reprints and in advertisements in other works of Lewis Carroll. The reprint dates appear to be more reliable.

The first reprint was May 1876. Copies are identical to the first edition, apart from re-spacing on the title-page to accommodate the number of the 'thousand'. Copies have been seen with 'Twelfth', 'Thirteenth' and 'Fourteenth thousand' (all below HENRY HOLIDAY, and in lower case).

The second reprint was in December 1876. The binding is totally different. It resembles the style of the 'Alice' books in being in red cloth, with three parallel lines round the border, and gilt roundels on the front and back covers - the front has the Bellman, the back the Beaver, this roundel being slightly smaller in size. The advertisements are updated. Copies have been seen with 'Seventeenth' and 'Eighteenth thousand' on the title-page (in upper-case italics). A copy is also known with no number of thousand stated. I think it likely that the 'sixteenth thousand' was also part of this reprint.

In 1883, the book went out of print. This was doubtless allowed to happen as this was the year of publication of 'Rhyme? and Reason?', and the 'Hunting of the Snark' was included in full, with the Holiday illustrations.

In 1890 however, we again see 'The Hunting of the Snark' being advertised - as the '19th thousand'. The reprint was in fact dated July 1890. The pictorial cover of the first edition returns, but in gold on red instead of black on buff. The number of the 'thousand' is not on the title-page.

Reprints followed in December 1890, 1891, and 1893. By this time the advertisements had been dropped from the end (though I have seen a copy of the 1893 reprint which does have the advertisements - but no later one)

Reprinted again in 1894, 1895, 1896 and 1897. It was with this last reprint that the size was increased slightly in height - the pages by ¼", the covers by ¼"; the increase matches the similarly increased size of the new editions of the 'Alice' books in 1897.

Reprinted again in 1897, 1898, 1899, 1900, 1903 and 1906 - where the end papers are white (this may have first occurred in 1903, but no earlier). Advertisements in other works of Carroll suggest that this is the 25th thousand. Again, and possibly finally, reprinted in 1910.

The price of the first edition was 3/6. The 16th thousand (probably part of the 2nd reprint) was being advertised at 3/6 in 1877; but in 1878, the 18th thousand was quoted at 4/6. The last reprint remained in print until 1920, the price rising to 6/- in 1918.

2

The Listing of the Snark, 1974:2.

MACMILLAN - THE MINIATURE EDITIONS

This was the edition that 'took over' from the standard edition. First published in October 1910. The format is that of the miniature editions of the 'Alice' books - the front cover has the Bellman roundel (as the 2nd. reprint of the standard edition), but the back cover is blank; the parallel lines round the borders are in blind only, but in gilt on the spine. The cloth is red. The Handbook collates it as (eights) 12mo., Macmillans always as Pott 8vo.

Issued in a dust-wrapper, but I have not seen a specimen. The dust-wrapper, however, for the 8th reprint (1931) is in blue on a white paper - the front cover has the Bellman roundel, the back the advertisements, the flaps are blank. The dust-wrapper for the 9th reprint (1935) is in red on white - the front cover has the illustration for the Baker's Tale, the back is blank, and the front flap has the advertisements, the back flap being blank.

The advertisements at the end of Carroll's works through the years 1910 to 1918 give the number of 'thousands'. As with the earlier reprints of the standard edition, these numbers are not reliable. For the record, advertisements in the 1st. reprint, November 1910 state '10th thousand', those in the second reprint, 1911, '15th thousand'; this remains the same until 1918 when it rises to '20th thousand'; thereafter the number is not stated. 'Alice's Adventures', on the other hand, in the 1912 reprint has '10th thousand', and 'Looking-Glass' similarly. Thereafter, all agree. The dates of the reprints are again more reliable.

These were in November 1910, 1911, 1913, 1916, 1920, 1924, 1928, 1931 and 1935. The price of the first edition was 1s. In 1918 it rose to 1/6; in 1921 to 2s; in 1942 to 2/6. The latest date I have seen it still advertised is 1948.

The 1928 issue was the first where an alternative binding was offered - Ecrase morocco, at 5s. This is pale orange with a gilt roundel on the front cover of the Baker taken from the illustration on p.5. The 1931 issue, and subsequent ones, were offered in another binding also - Ledura leather-cloth, at 3s. (rising to 3/6 in 1942), the alternatives are much less commonly seen.

MACMILLAN - CARDINAL SERIES

The Handbook states that the original edition was reissued in July and October 1929 - in Macmillan's Cardinal Series. I have no further details of this.

AMERICAN EDITIONS

1876 - published by James R. Osgood, Boston. With the Holiday illustrations, 24mo. Probably produced by a photographic process from the English Edition - hence its small size. There was a second edition in 1877.

1890 - Macmillan, New York. Said to be 12mo. Possibly timed to coincide with the new reprint in England. Reprinted in 1891.

3

The Listing of the Snark, 1974:3.

1897 — published by Van Vechten & Ellis, Warsaw, Wisconsin. A limited edition of 99 numbered copies. Fully described by Stan Marx in 'Journal of the Long Island Book Collectors' No. 1 1969. Uncut, bound
in vellum boards, decorated in red and black. Text is black with
wide, red decorative borders. Illustrations by Gardner C. Teall,
with a 'Word by way of Palliation' by William H. Ellis.
A 'de luxe edition' was issued in 1910 (see 'The Annotated Snark').

1898 — Macmillan, New York. Plain red cloth, white end-papers, no advertisements. Printed on one side of the leaf only, i.e. the book has
53 leaves, not pages as stated in the Handbook.
Reprinted in 1899, 1902 and 1908.
Also reprinted in 1910 and 1914 — where the lettering on the binding
is white on green. Last reprinted in 1927.

189? — A. L. Burt, New York. Illustrated by Holiday. 'Sylvie and Bruno' is
also included (following 'The Snark').

1901 — A. L. Burt, New York, 12mo.

1903 — Harper and Bros. Illustrated by Peter Newell. Tall 8vo. Cream boards,
decorated and lettered in gilt, top edge gilt, other edges uncut.
Coloured frontispiece, monochrome plates. Full title is 'The Hunting
of the Snark & Other Poems & Verses'. Issued in a green dust-wrapper.
Also issued in a green binding. Reprinted in 1906.

1906 — Putnam, New York. 12mo.

1909 — Altemus, Philadelphia.

1927 — Kahoe and Speith, Yellow Springs, Ohio.

1939 — Peter Pauper Press, Mount Vernon, New York. Illustrated by Paul
Cobbledick. In decorated green boards, boxed as issued. Pictorial
title page in green, sepia and black. Each page decorated in green
and sepia.
There is another issue, undated. I do not know which, if either, has
precedence. It is limited to 1450 copies. Grey boards, with darker-
grey postage-stamp-size illustrations of the characters. Black on red-
paper-label on the spine with title. Pictorial title-page in red, grey
and black. Each page decorated, the colours changing in rotation for
each fit — grey/red, grey/green, grey/orange, grey/blue.

1952 — Peter Pauper Press: and Mayflower Publishing Co. and Vision Press,
New York. Full title is 'The Hunting of the Snark, and Other Nonsense
Verses'. A 'Collector's Presentation Edition'.

1962 — 'The Annotated Snark', with introduction and Notes by Martin Gardner:
Simon and Schuster, New York. Half-cloth in buff, with paper-board
sides in dark brown. Cream dust-wrapper printed in black, red and
brown. (see below for English reprints).
To misquote the Handbook, this volume could be called "The complete
apotheosis of Snarkolatry".

1966 — Pantheon, New York. Illustrated by Kelly Oechsli.

1973 — 'The Snark Puzzle Book', by Martin Gardner: Simon and Schuster, New
York. Decorated yellow cloth, dust-wrapper in turquoise, with 'bell-
buoy' design.

4

The Listing of the Snark, 1974:4.

OTHER ENGLISH EDITIONS

1940 - 'The Hunting of the Snark and Other Verses': Oxford University Press,
London. Number 2 in the series 'Chameleon Books'. Unillustrated.
Decorated paper on boards, with matching dust-wrapper, the title here
is phrased a little differently from the title-page - 'The Hunting of
the Snark & Other Lewis Carroll Verses'.
Reprinted in 1946 and 1949.

1941 - Illustrated by Mervyn Peake: Chatto & Windus, London. There are two
issues of the first edition; again I do not know which has precedence
(if either). The more elaborate is large 8vo., bound in pink cloth on
boards, with gilt lettering on the spine. Issued in a grey dust-wrapper reproducing on the front the title-page illustration and on the back
the illustration from p.40 (enlarged).
The other first edition is the one that led on to the reprints issued
up to the present time. The contents are very similar, but the title-
page design is reduced in size; the remainder of the text, and illustrations however are of an identical size (the pink cloth edition
therefore has much wider margins). The page facing the title-page has
A ZODIAC BOOK/Published by/Chatto & Windus (all in italics). Issued in
yellow paper on boards, with the front cover reproducing in black the
illustration from p.19, the back cover the illustration from p.26 with
the title and recurring refrain from the poem.
Reprinted in 1941 and 1942.

The next issue was in 1948. It is still called a Zodiac Book, but
there is no reference to any previous edition. On the reverse side of
the title-page it states 'Published by Lighthouse Books Ltd. and distributed by Chatto & Windus, London', the name of the publisher is removed from the page facing the title-page. Below the verse on the back
cover, the publisher is also removed, but the price (2s) is added.
Otherwise it is virtually identical to the 1941 edition.

A new edition was published in 1953. Though slightly larger, it is
still very similar to foregoing ones; the binding is now blank yellow
paper (simulating cloth) on boards, with the title on the spine in
gilt. A dust-wrapper copies the style of the covers of previous editions, except that there is nothing below the verse on the back cover.
On the reverse of the title-page it does state '4th impression'. This
is incorrect - if it is to be called an impression at all, it should
be the 5th: copies from later dates have it more correctly.

2nd impression of this edition was 1958, 3rd impression 1964. These
are again incorrectly stated to be 5th and 6th impressions.

4th and 5th impressions followed in 1969 and 1973. These now have a
correct statement about editions and impressions - to be found as usual on the reverse of the title-page.

The prices reflect the modern trend of inflation - in 1948 the price
was 2s., in 1964 5s., and in 1969 10s. (1973 50p½). Compare those
with the remarkably stable prices of the early Macmillan editions.

5

The Listing of the Snark, 1974:5.

In 1960, there was a special issue; it is slightly smaller, but the contents are similar, and the text etc. identical in size. It is bound in limp beige cloth, the front cover has in black the title and part of the illustration from p.45; the back cover has the title and the illustration from p.10, and at the bottom - THE REPRINT SOC-IETY - LONDON. On the reverse of the title page is: 'This edition published by the Reprint Society Ltd. by arrangement with Chatto & Windus Ltd.'

1966 - Illustrated by Peter Vos: De Roos, Utrecht. A limited edition of 175 numbered copies.

1967 - 'The Annotated Snark': Penguin Books Ltd. The first English Edition: with a new preface.
Reprinted in 1973, with revisions, and extended bibliography.

1970 - Illustrated by Helen Oxenbury: Heinemann, London. Illustrations in colour and monochrome. Pictorial cloth binding, with matching dust-wrapper.

TRANSLATIONS

French

1929 - translated by Louis Aragon: Hours Press (Miss Nancy Cunard), Chapelle - Reanville, Eure. A limited edition of 505 numbered copies signed by the translator, five on Japon. But an un-numbered copy of Japon is also known.
Reprinted by P. Seghers, Paris in 1949 and 1962. The latter is bound in stiff wrappers, with a picture on the front cover in green and pur-ple by Mario Prassinos.

1940 - translated by Henri Parisot: Librairie Jose Corti. A limited edition of 255 copies - 250 on Alfa, and 5 on Madagascar. In paper wrappers, unillustrated.

1945 - translated by Henri Parisot: P. Seghers, Paris. Also includes 'de Fantasmagorie et de Poeta fit Non Nascitur'.

1946 - translated by Henri Parisot, 'revue et corrigee', illustrations by Gisele Prassinos: Fontaine, Paris. Full title - 'La Chasse au Snark et autres poemes' (which are the two above plus 'Le Morse et le Charpentier, Assis sur une Barriere et Jabberwocky')

1948 - translated by Florence Gillian and Guy Levis Mano: G.L.M., Paris. A limited edition of 1080 copies. It includes the English text

1950 - traduction nouvelle de Henri Parisot, Illustrations de Max Ernst: Editions Premieres, Paris.

1952 - translation by Henri Parisot, included in his biography of Lewis Carr-oll (in the series 'Poetes d'Aujourd 'hui'). One of the Ernst illus-trations is included.

1971 - translated by Henri Parisot, included with his translation of 'Through the Looking-Glass': Aubier-Flammarion, Paris. Includes the Ernst illus-trations.

6

The Listing of the Snark, 1974:6.

I have copies of the Parisot translations of 1940, 1952 and 1971.
All are different. I suspect that he revised it more often than
he admits to.

Latin

1934 – translated by P. H. Brinton: Macmillan, London and Toronto. In Vergil-
ian Hexameters.

1936 – translated by H. D. Watson: Shakespeare Head Press, sold by Basil
Blackwell, Oxford. With a foreword by Gilbert Murray. Unillustrated.
In dark blue cloth with title on the front cover and spine in gilt. The
translation is in Latin Elegiacs, and was directly inspired by Brinton's
translation. The English text is also included, and a number of other
poems by the translater, with their Latin translations also.

Italian

1945 – translated by Cesare Vico Lodovici, illustrated by Ketty Castellucci:
Magi-Spinetti. Title – 'le caccia allo Snarco'.

Swedish

1959 – illustrations by Tove Jansen: Albert Bouniers Forlag, Stockholm.
Title – 'Snarkjagten'.

Danish

1963 – translated by Christopher Maaløe: Det Schönbergske Forlag, Copenhagen.
English text is included. The cover has a photo reproduction of a fab-
ric picture of a Snark with a bathing-machine with Union Jack wheels.
Title – 'Snarkjagten'.

German

1968 – translated by Klaus Reichert: Insel Verlag, Frankfurt am Main. English
text is included. The volume matches the edition of 'Alice's Adventures in Wonderland' and 'Letters to Child Friends', published in 1967.
Paper on boards, the covers are in the style of the first edition, but
in purple on lime-green; a paper label is added on the front and spine,
with the title. The volume includes all Holiday's pictures. Title:
'Die Jagd nach dem Snark'.

COLLECTED EDITIONS INCLUDING THE SNARK

I am including this section for the sake of completeness: unlike the previous
sections, I do not claim that it is comprehensive, though I hope that most are
in fact included. Certain volumes, which properly belong here, have been listed or mentioned earlier – 'Rhyme? and Reason?' because it is vital to the narrative of events; the Parisot translations for the sake of clarity; and a number because the title presents the Snark as the main feature of the book – the
189? Burt edition, the 1902 Peter Newell, the 1952 Peter Pauper, the 1940
Chameleon Books edition, and the 1936 Watson Latin Translation.

The books here are only cited in their first editions: in chronological order –

7

The Listing of the Snark, 1974:7.

1. Alice's Adventures in Wonderland, Through the Looking-Glass and the Hunting of the Snark (introduction by Alexander Woollcott): The Modern Library, Boni & Liveright, New York 1924.

2. Alice in Wonderland, Through the Looking-Glass and Other Comic Pieces: Everyman's Library, Dent/Dutton, London/New York 1929.

3. The Collected Verse of Lewis Carroll: E.P. Dutton & Co., New York 1929.

4. Alice in Wonderland with the Hunting of the Snark and Poems from Sylvie and Bruno. (ed. Guy N. Pocock): The Kings Treasuries of Literature, J. M. Dent 1930.

5. The Lewis Carroll Book (ed. Richard Herrick): The Dial Press, New York 1931.

6. The Collected Verse of Lewis Carroll: Macmillan, London 1932.

7. Logical Nonsense: The Works of Lewis Carroll (ed. Philip C. Blackburn and Lional White): G. P. Putnam's Sons, New York 1934.

8. Nonsensibus .... by D. B. Wyndham Lewis: Methuen, London 1936.
(reprinted as separate Fits throughout the book).

9. Poems selected from the Works of Lewis Carroll: Macmillan, London 1939.

10. The Complete Works of Lewis Carroll (Introduced by Alexander Woollcott): Random House, New York, Nonesuch Press, London 1939.
(the introduction is identical to the one in 1.)

11. Poets of the English Language Vol. 5, Tennyson to Yeats (ed. W.H. Auden and Norman Holmes Pearson): The Viking Press 1950.

12. Alice's Adventures in Wonderland, Through the Looking-Glass and other Writings (introduction by Robin Deniston): Collins, London and Glasgow 1954.

13. The Book of Nonsense by many authors (ed. Roger Lancelyn Green): Children's Illustrated Classics, Dent, London 1956.

14. Lewis Carroll, Nonsense Verse: Pocket Poets, Edward Hulton, London 1959.

15. The Silver Treasury of Light Verse (ed. Oscar Williams): A Mentor Book, The New American Library c. 1957.

16. Alice's Adventures in Wonderland, Through the Looking-Glass, and the Hunting of the Snark: A Nonesuch Cygnet, the Nonesuch Press, London 1963. (published under the Bodley Head imprint 1974).

17. The Works of Lewis Carroll (ed. Roger Lancelyn Green): Spring Books, Paul Hamlyn, London 1966.

18. Alice in Wonderland (ed. Donald J. Gray): a Norton Critical Edition, W. W. Norton & Co., New York 1971

8

The Listing of the Snark, 1974:8.

PROJECTED EDITIONS

We look forward with keen anticipation to the promised new illustrated version by Byron Sewell.

We have also heard it rumoured that Ralph Steadman is planning an illustrated version - as the natural follow-up to his 'Alice's Adventures in Wonderland' 1967, and 'Through the Looking-Glass' 1972.

And can we hope that Macmillans will issue a centenary edition in 1976?

References

Catalogue of the Columbia University Exhibition, April 1932.

Lewis Carroll, par Henri Parisot: Poetes d'Aujourd hui, Pierre Seghers, Paris 1952.

The Parrish Collection of Carrolliana, by Warren Weaver: Princeton University Library Chronicle, Winter 1956.

The Lewis Carroll Handbook, revised by Roger Lancelyn Green: Oxford University Press, London 1962.

Alice in Many Tongues, by Warren Weaver: University of Wisconsin Press, Madison 1964.

Alice One Hundred, by R. D. Hilton Smith: Adelphi Bookshop Ltd., Victoria, B.C. 1966.

A Century of Annotations to the Lewis Carroll Handbook, by Denis N. Crutch: Yellow Hammer Press, London 1967.

9

The Listing of the Snark, 1974:9.

Issued in a limited edition of 80 signed copies

of which this is No. 67

Designed by Drucella Starkey

Covers by The Regent Press, Church Gresley

The Listing of the Snark, 1974:10.

Copyright page.

THE LISTING OF THE SNARK

Corrections and Additions - March 1975

Corrections

page 1   The copy with 'inverted head on the cover' is a copy of 'Sylvie
         and Bruno'.

         It now seems certain that the First Edition numbered 10,000.
         Copies are known with 'eleventh thousand' on the title page.

page 2   A copy of the 'seventeenth thousand' is known in the early bind-
         ing. It seems likely that the price rise and the change of bind-
         ing occurred during the binding of the 17th thousand.

         The earliest of the resumed advertisements (1899) state that the
         book is in the 18th thousand. Possibly the old stock was first
         sold off, before the 19th thousand in the new binding was prepared.

         Copies of the reprints for 1897 and 1908 (a reprint I omitted) are
         known with advertisements.

page 3   The dust-wrapper for the First Miniature Edition is yellow paper
         covered with a close design based on the Macmillan motif, with
         lettering in black; the back cover has the advertisements, and
         the flaps are blank.

         The 1916 reprint also states '20th thousand'.

page 5   'Chameleon Books' edition - the end papers are designed by Malcolm
         Easton, and show 7 of the Snark Crew. The First Edition is dated
         1939.

page 8   The date of the Random House 'Complete Works' is 1936, and the
         Spring Books 'Works' is 1965.

Additions

                              TRANSLATIONS

French

1962 -   translated by Henri Parisot: Jean-Jacques Pauvert, Editeur, Con-
         tains Holiday illustrations, blue paper covers with the title in
         black, reproduction of First Edition cover on front and back in
         black and white.

         A limited edition of 1,999 numbered copies, 1-30 on Pur Fil Du
         Marais.

The Listing of the Snark: Corrections and Additions, 1975:1.

German

1968 – Die Jagd nach dem Schnark: Agonie in acht Krampfen: Manus Press, Stuttgart.
Original lithographie von Max Ernst.

COLLECTED EDITIONS INCLUDING THE SNARK

1. The Humorous Verse of Lewis Carroll (ed. J.E. Morpurgo): in the series "Crown Classics", Grey Walls Press, London 1950.

2. Lewis Carroll's Alice in Wonderland and Other Favorites: Pocket Books, Inc., New York 1951 (there is also a Canadian printing).

3. The World of Victorian Humor, (ed. Harold Orel): Appleton-Century-Crofts, Inc., New York 1961.

4. The Oxford Book of Nineteenth Century Verse (ed. John Hayward): Oxford University Press, London 1964.

PROJECTED EDITIONS

An Edition with new illustrations by Harold Jones is to be published in May 1975, in a limited edition of 750 copies, signed and numbered by the artist, at £15 (cloth), £40 (leather) by the Whittington Press.

The Byron Sewell Edition has now been announced – a limited edition of 250 numbered copies, each signed by Byron Sewell, published by Catalpa Press, London 1974. With an Introduction by Martin Gardner. Price £25.

There is more definite news of the Ralph Steadman version – it is to be published by Michael Dempsey, London.

–––––––––––

The Listing of the Snark: Corrections and Additions, 1975:2.

140

SOURCES

Alice's Adventures in Wonderland: The Evertype definitive edition,
by Lewis Carroll, 2016

Alice's Adventures in Wonderland, illus. June Lornie, 2013

Alice's Adventures in Wonderland, illus. Mathew Staunton, 2015

Alice's Adventures in Wonderland, illus. Harry Furniss, 2016

Alice's Adventures in Wonderland, illus. J. Michael Rolen, 2017

Through the Looking-Glass and What Alice Found There,
by Lewis Carroll, 2009

The Nursery "Alice", by Lewis Carroll, 2015

Alice's Adventures under Ground, by Lewis Carroll, 2009

The Hunting of the Snark, by Lewis Carroll, 2010

SEQUELS

A New Alice in the Old Wonderland, by Anna Matlack Richards, 2009

New Adventures of Alice, by John Rae, 2010

Alice Through the Needle's Eye, by Gilbert Adair, 2012

Wonderland Revisited and the Games Alice Played There,
by Keith Sheppard, 2009

Alice and the Boy who Slew the Jabberwock,
by Allan William Parkes, 2016

Alice and the Missing Chapter,
New chapters by fourteen authors, edited by Michael Everson, 2024

SPELLING

Alice's Adventures in Wonderland,
Retold in words of one Syllable by Mrs J. C. Gorham, 2010

𐐘𐐶𐐮𐑅'𐑆 𐐟𐐼𐑂𐐯𐑌𐐽𐐲𐑉𐑆 𐐮𐑌 𐐎𐐲𐑌𐐼𐐲𐑉𐑊𐐲𐑌𐐼 (Alis'z Advenchurz in
Wundurland), *Alice* printed in the Deseret Alphabet, 2014

𐐜 𐐏𐐲𐑌𐐻𐐮𐑍 𐐲𐑂 𐐼 𐐝𐑌𐐪𐑉𐐿 (Dh Hunting uv dh Snark),
The Hunting of the Snark printed in the Deseret Alphabet, 2016

Lᶑᴐ ꭕ Lꟼᴐᴢᴎ-Ꮎᵢᴚᴤ ᴬᴺᴰ Ψᴜꟼᵢ ᴠᵢᴚᴤ Pᴐᴎᴅ ꭎᴬᵠ
(Thru dh Lüking-Glas and Hwut Alis Fawnd Dher),
Looking-Glass printed in the Deseret Alphabet, 2016

Alice's Adventures in Wonderland,
Alice printed in Dyslexic-Friendly fonts, 2015

Through the Looking-Glass and What Alice Found There,
Looking-Glass printed in Dyslexic-Friendly fonts, 2020

∧₋ᴵᶜᴱ'ᔕ ∀ᴆ/Ɛᴵᴵᴵ ᴶᴿᴱᔕ ᴵᴵ∧ ᴆᴶ ᔕ₋Ɛᴧᶜ ᴠ/ᴑᴵᴶᴱᴿ₋∧ᴵᴵᴆ,
Alice printed in a font that simulates Dyslexia, 2015

ᕈᴸ ᕈᴸᴋᕮᴩ � ᕈᴩᕈᕈᕈ ꟼ ᴧᴊᴴᴵᴵꓯ ᕈᴴᕈ ᕈᕆꓯᴵ ᴴᴵᴸ ᕈᕈᴒ (Ælɪꜱᴇᴢ
Ædvéntʃuɹz ɪn Wɐndʊɹlænd), *Alice* printed in the Ewellic Alphabet, 2013

'Ælɪsɪz Əd'ventʃəz ɪn 'Wʌndə,lænd,
Alice printed in the International Phonetic Alphabet, 2014

Alɪs'z Advnĕrz ɪn Wunᶁland, *Alice* printed in the Ñspel orthography, 2015

˙.ᴸ₋ᴄ⌐ᴶᴦ ˙.ᴶ˸⌐ᴜᴘ˙˙ꓕᴦ ₋ᴜ ᴥᴐᴜᴶ⌐ᴒᴸ˙.ᴜᴶ,
Alice printed in the Nyctographic Square Alphabet, 2011

ᴦ ᴨ˙˙ᴜᴶ₋ᴜᴸ ᴑᴦ ᴦ ᴦᴜ˙.ᴒᴦ.,
The Hunting of the Snark printed in the Nyctographic Square Alphabet, 2024

Alice's Adventures in Wonderland,
Alice printed in Pitman New Era Shorthand, forthcoming

Alice's Adventures in Wonderland, *Alice* printed in QR Codes, 2018

.ɹcɪʃ'ɹ ɾᵤɾᴜᴵlʮɔʒ ɪɪ ·ɾᴜᴦₒcɹʮ (Alɪs'əz ədventjuːrz ɪn Wʌndərlænd),
Alice printed in the Shaw Alphabet, 2013

Alɪsɪᴢ Advenᴄɜrᴢ ɪn Wundɹland,
Alice printed in the Unifon Alphabet, 2014

ᴐᵻꓫ᙭ᴀᕳᴴᴐꟼᴴᴐꓜ ᵻꟼᴴᴐꟼᴀꟼᴥ ᕳᵻᴀᕈ (Alɪz kalandjai Csodaországban),
The Hungarian *Alice* printed in Old Hungarian script, tr. Anikó Szilágyi, 2016

SCHOLARSHIP

Elucidating Alice: A Textual Commentary on *Alice's Adventures in
Wonderland*, by Selwyn Goodacre, 2015

Reflecting Alice: A Textual Commentary
on *Through the Looking-Glass*, by Selwyn Goodacre, 2021.

SEWELLIANA

Sun-hee's Adventures Under the Land of Morning Calm,
by Victoria J. Sewell & Byron W. Sewell, 2016

선희의 조용한 아침의 나라 모험기 (Seonhuiui Joyonghan Achim-ui Nala
Moheomgi), *Sun-hee* in Korean, tr. Miyeong Kang, forthcoming

Alix's Adventures in Wonderland:
Lewis Carroll's Nightmare, by Byron W. Sewell, 2011

Aloþk's Adventures in Goatland, by Byron W. Sewell, 2011

Alice's Bad Hair Day in Wonderland, by Byron W. Sewell, 2013

The Carrollian Tales of Inspector Spectre, by Byron W. Sewell, 2011

The Annotated Alice in Nurseryland, by Byron W. Sewell, 2016

The Haunting of the Snarkasbord, by Alison Tannenbaum,
Byron W. Sewell, Charlie Lovett, & August A. Imholtz, Jr, 2012

The Millennium Snark Trilogy, by Byron W. Sewell, 2024

Snarkmaster, by Byron W. Sewell, 2012

In the Boojum Forest, by Byron W. Sewell, 2014

Murder by Boojum, by Byron W. Sewell, 2014

Close Encounters of the Snarkian Kind, by Byron W. Sewell, 2016

TRANSLATIONS

Кайкалдыҥ Јеринде Алисала болгон учуралдар (Kaykaldiń Cerinde
Alisala bolgon uçuraldar), *Alice* in Altai, tr. Küler Tepukov, 2016

Alice's Adventures in An Appalachian Wonderland,
Alice in Appalachian English, tr. Byron & Victoria Sewell, 2012

Սնարքի Որսը (Snark'i Orsě),
The Hunting of the Snark in Eastern Armenian,
tr. Alexander Kalantaryan & Artak Kalantaryan, forthcoming

Ալիս Հրաշալիքներու Աշխարհին Մէջ (Alis Hrashalik'neru Ashkharhin Mēch),
Alice in Western Armenian, tr. Yervant Gobelean, forthcoming

Patimatli ali Alice tu Vāsilia ti Ciudii,
Alice in Aromanian, tr. Mariana Bara, 2015

Элисәнең Сәйерстандағы мажаралары (Älisäneñ Säyerstandağı majaraları), *Alice* in Bashkir, tr. Güzäl Sitdykova, 2017

Алесіны прыгоды ў Цудазем'і (Alesiny pryhody u Tsudazem'i), *Alice* in Belarusian, tr. Max Ščur, 2016

На тым баку Люстра і што там напаткала Алесю (Na tym baku Liustra i shto tam napatkala Alesiu), *Looking-Glass* in Belarusian, tr. Max Ščur, 2016

Снаркаловы (Snarkalovy), *The Hunting of the Snark* in Belarusian, tr. Max Ščur, forthcoming

Troioù-kaer Alis e Vro ar Marzhoù, *Alice* in Breton, tr. Herve Kerrain, forthcoming

Crystal's Adventures in A Cockney Wonderland, *Alice* in Cockney Rhyming Slang, tr. Charlie Lovett, 2015

Aventurs Alys in Pow an Anethow, *Alice* in Cornish, tr. Nicholas Williams, 2015

Aventurs Alys in Pow an Anethow Dyllans Dywyêthek Kernowek-Sowsnek, *Alice* in Cornish, bilingual edition, tr. Nicholas Williams, 2021

Alice's Ventures in Wunderland, *Alice* in Cornu-English, tr. Alan M. Kent, 2015

Maries Hændelser i Vidunderlandet, *Alice* in Danish, tr. D.G., forthcoming

آلیس در سرزمین عجایب (Âlis dar Sarzamin-e Ajâyeb), *Alice* in Dari, tr. Rahman Arman, 2015

Äventyrä Alice i Underlandä, *Alice* in Elfdalian, tr. Inga-Britt Petersson, 2022

La Aventuroj de Alicio en Mirlando, *Alice* in Esperanto, tr. E. L. Kearney (1910), 2009

La Aventuroj de Alico en Mirlando, *Alice* in Esperanto, tr. Donald Broadribb, 2012

Trans la Spegulo kaj kion Alico trovis tie, *Looking-Glass* in Esperanto, tr. Donald Broadribb, 2012

Les Aventures d'Alice au pays des merveilles, *Alice* in French, tr. Henri Bué, 2015

Les Aventures d'Alice au pays des merveilles,
Alice in French, tr. Henri Bué, illus. Mathew Staunton, 2015

De aventoeren fan Alice yn Wûnderlân,
Alice in West Frisian, tr. Tiny Mulder, 2024

ელისის თავგადასავალი საოცრებათა ქვეყანაში (Elisis t'avgadasavali
saoc'rebat a k'veqanaši), *Alice* in Georgian, tr. Giorgi Gokieli, 2016

Alice's Abenteuer im Wunderland,
Alice in German, tr. Antonie Zimmermann, 2010

Die Lissel ehr Erlebnisse im Wunnerland,
Alice in Palantine German, tr. Franz Schlosser, 2013

Der Alice ihre Obmteier im Wunderlaund,
Alice in Viennese German, tr. Hans Werner Sokop, 2012

Balþos Gadedeis Aþalhaidais in Sildaleikalanda,
Alice in Gothic, tr. David Alexander Carlton, 2015

Nā Hana Kupanaha a ʻĀleka ma ka ʻĀina Kamahaʻo,
Alice in Hawaiian, tr. R. Keao NeSmith, 2017

Nā Hana Kupanaha a ʻĀleka ma ka ʻĀina Kamahaʻo
Kope ʻōlelo Hawaiʻi-ʻōlelo Pelekānia,
Alice in Hawaiian, bilingual edition, tr. R. Keao NeSmith, 2022

Ma Loko o ke Aniani Kū a me ka Mea i Loaʻa iā ʻĀleka
ma Laila, *Looking-Glass* in Hawaiian, tr. R. Keao NeSmith, 2017

Alíz kalandjai Csodaországban,
Alice in Hungarian, tr. Anikó Szilágyi, 2013

Ævintýri Lísu í Undralandi, *Alice* in Icelandic, tr. Þórarinn Eldjárn, 2013

L'Aventuri di Alicia en Marvelia, *Alice* in Ido, tr. Gonçalo Neves, 2020

Le Aventuras de Alice in le Pais del Meravilias,
Alice in Interlingua, tr. Rodrigo Guerra, 2020

Eachtra Eibhlíse i dTír na nIontas,
Alice in Irish, tr. Pádraig Ó Cadhla (1922), 2015

Eachtraí Eilíse i dTír na nIontas, *Alice* in Irish, tr. Nicholas Williams, 2007

Eachtraí Eilíse i dTír na nIontas: Eagrán Dátheangach Gaeilge-Béarla,
Alice in Irish, bilingual edition, tr. tr. Nicholas Williams, 2022

Lastall den Scáthán agus a bhFuair Eilís Ann Roimpi,
Looking-Glass in Irish, tr. Nicholas Williams, 2009

Le Avventure di Alice nel Paese delle Meraviglie,
Alice in Italian, tr. Teodorico Pietrocòla Rossetti, 2010

Alis Advencha ina Wandalan,
Alice in Jamaican Creole, tr. Tamirand Nnena De Lisser, 2016

L's Aventuthes d'Alice en Êmèrvil'lie,
Alice in Jèrriais, tr. Geraint Williams, 2012

L'Travèrs du Mitheux et chein qu'Alice y dêmuchit,
Looking-Glass in Jèrriais, tr. Geraint Williams, 2012

Алисэ Телъыджэщlым зэрыщыlар (Alisė Telʺydzhèshchḩym
zėryshchyḩar), *Alice* in Kabardian, tr. Murat Temyr & Murat Brat, 2020

Алиса Къужур Дунияны Къыдырады (Alisa Qujur Duniyanı
Qıdıradı), *Alice* in Karachay-Balkar, tr. Magomet Gekki, 2019

Элисэнің ғажайып елдегі басынан кешкендері (Älïsäniñ ğajayıp
eldegi basınan keşkenderi), *Alice* in Kazakh, tr. Fatima Moldashova, 2016

Алисаның Хайхастар Чирінзер чорығы (Alïsanıñ Hayhastar Çïrinzer
çorığı), *Alice* in Khakas, tr. Maria Çertykova, 2017

Алисакöд Шемöсмуын лоöмторъяс (Alisaköd Šemösmuyn loömtorʺias),
Alice in Komi-Zyrian, tr. Evgenii Tsypanov & Elena Eltsova, 2018

Алисанын Кызыктар Өлкөсундөгу укмуштуу окуялары
(Alisanın Kızıktar Ölkösündögü ukmuştuu okuyaları),
Alice in Kyrgyz, tr. Aida Egemberdieva, 2016

Las Aventuras de Alisia en el Paiz de las Maraviyas,
Alice in Ladino, tr. Avner Perez, 2016

לאס אבﬞיﬞבﬞמﬞוראﬞס דﬞי אﬞליﬞדﬞייﬞה אﬞיﬞך אﬞיﬞל פﬞאﬞאﬞיﬞס דﬞי לﬞאﬞס מﬞאﬞראﬞבﬞיﬞליﬞיﬞאﬞס
(Las Aventuras de Alisia en el Paiz de las Maraviyas),
Alice in Ladino, tr. Avner Perez, 2016

Alisis pīdzeivuojumi Breinumu zemē,
Alice in Latgalian, tr. Evika Muizniece, 2015

Alicia in Terrā Mīrābilī, *Alice* in Latin, tr. Clive Harcourt Carruthers, 2018

Alicia in Terrā Mīrābilī: Ēditiō Bilinguis Latīna et Anglica,
Alice in Latin, bilingual edition, tr. Clive Harcourt Carruthers, 2021

Aliciae per Speculum Trānsitus (Quaeque Ibi Invēnit),
Looking-Glass in Latin, tr. Clive Harcourt Carruthers, forthcoming

Alisa-ney Aventuras in Divalanda, *Alice* in Lingua de Planeta (Lidepla),
tr. Anastasia Lysenko & Dmitry Ivanov, 2014

La aventuras de Alisia en la pais de mervelias,
Alice in Lingua Franca Nova, tr. Simon Davies, 2012

Alice ehr Eventüürn in't Wunnerland,
Alice in Low German, tr. Reinhard F. Hahn, 2010

Contoyrtyssyn Ealish ayns Cheer ny Yindyssyn,
Alice in Manx, tr. Brian Stowell, 2010

Ko Ngā Takahanga i a Ārihi i Te Ao Mīharo,
Alice in Māori, tr. Tom Roa, 2015

Dee Erläwnisse von Alice em Wundalaund,
Alice in Mennonite Low German, tr. Jack Thiessen, 2012

Auanturiou adelis en Bro an Marthou,
Alice in Middle Breton, tr. Herve Le Bihan & Herve Kerrain, forthcoming

The Aventures of Alys in Wondyr Lond,
Alice in Middle English, tr. Brian S. Lee, 2013

Þurh þe Loking-Glas and What Alys Founde Þere,
Looking-Glass in Middle English, tr. Brian S. Lee, forthcoming

L'Avventure d'Alice 'int' 'o Paese d' 'e Maraveglie,
Alice in Neapolitan, tr. Roberto D'Ajello, 2016

Attravierzo 'o specchio e cchello c'Alice ce truvaie,
Looking-Glass in Neapolitan, tr. Roberto D'Ajello, 2019

L'Aventuros de Alis in Marvoland, *Alice* in Neo, tr. Ralph Midgley, 2013

Elises Eventyr i Undernes Land: den første norske *Alice:*
Elise's Adventures in the Land of Wonders: the first Norwegian *Alice,*
Alice in Norwegian, ed. & tr. Anne Kristin Lande, 2022

Alice sine opplevingar i Eventyrlandet,
Alice in Nynorsk, tr. Sigrun Anny Røssbø, 2020

Æðelgyðe Ellendæda on Wundorlande,
Alice in Old English, tr. Peter S. Baker, 2015

La geste d'Aalis el Païs de Merveilles,
Alice in Old French, tr. May Plouzeau, 2017

Alitjilu Palyantja Tjuta Ngura Tjukurmankuntjala (Alitji's Adventures
in Dreamland), *Alice* in Pitjantjatjara, tr. Nancy Sheppard, forthcoming

Alitji's Adventures in Dreamland: An Aboriginal tale inspired by
Alice's Adventures in Wonderland, adapted by Nancy Sheppard, forthcoming

Alice Contada aos Mais Pequenos,
The Nursery "Alice" in Portuguese, tr., Rogério Miguel Puga, 2015

Aventurile lui Alice în Țara Minunilor,
Alice in Romanian, tr., Claudia E. Stoian, 2020

Aventurile Alisei în Țara Minunilor,
Alice in Bessarabian Romanian, tr., Tatiana Sima, forthcoming

Сыр Алиса Попэя кэ Чюдэнгири Пхув (Sir Alisa Popeja ke Čudengiri
Phuv), *Alice* in North Russian Romani, tr. Viktor Shapoval, 2018

Соня въ царствѣ дива (Sonia v tsarstvie diva): Sonja in a Kingdom of
Wonder, *Alice* in facsimile of the 1879 first Russian translation, 2013

Соня в царстве дива (Sonia v tsarstve diva),
An edition of the first Russian *Alice* in modern orthography, 2017

Приключения Алисы в Стране Чудес (Prikliucheniia Alisy v Strane
Chudes), *Alice* in Russian, tr. Yury Nesterenko, 2018

Приключения Алисы в Стране Чудес (Prikliucheniia Alisy v Strane
Chudes), *Alice* in Russian, bilingual edition, tr. Yury Nesterenko, 2022

Приключения Алисы в Стране Чудес (Prikliucheniia Alisy v Strane
Chudes), *Alice* in Russian, tr. Nina Demurova, 2020

Алиса в Стране Чудес (Alisa v Strane Chudes), *Alice* in Russian,
tr. A. Daktil' (Anatolii Frenkel'), 2022

Охота на Снарка (Okhota na Snarka),
The Hunting of the Snark in Russian, tr. Victor Fet, 2016

Ia Aventures as Alice in Daumsenland,
Alice in Sambahsa, tr. Olivier Simon, 2013

Ocolo id Specule ed Quo Alice Trohv Ter,
Looking-Glass in Sambahsa, tr. Olivier Simon, 2016

'O Tāfaoga a 'Ālise i le Nu'u o Mea Ofoofogia,
Alice in Samoan, tr. Luafata Simanu-Klutz, 2013

Eachdraidh Ealasaid ann an Tìr nan Iongantas,
Alice in Scottish Gaelic, tr. Moray Watson, 2012

Alice's Adventchers in Wunderland,
Alice in Scouse, tr. Marvin R. Sumner, 2015

Mbalango wa Alice eTikweni ra Swihlamariso,
Alice in Shangani, tr. Peniah Mabaso & Steyn Khesani Madlome, 2015

Ahlice's Aveenturs in Wunderlaant,
Alice in Border Scots, tr. Cameron Halfpenny, 2015

Alice's Mishanters in e Land o Farlies,
Alice in Caithness Scots, tr. Catherine Byrne, 2014

Alice's Advenchers in Wunnerlaund,
Alice in Fife Scots, tr. Tom Hubbard, 2024

Alice's Adventirs in Wunnerlaun,
Alice in Glaswegian Scots, tr. Thomas Clark, 2014

Ailice's Anters in Ferlielann,
Alice in North-East Scots (Doric), tr. Derrick McClure, 2012

Throwe the Keekin-Gless an Fit Ailice's Funn There,
Looking-Glass in North-East Scots (Doric), tr. Derrick McClure, 2021

Alice's Adventirs in Wonderlaand,
Alice in Shetland Scots, tr. Laureen Johnson, 2012

Ailice's Àventurs in Wunnerland,
Alice in Southeast Central Scots, tr. Sandy Fleemin, 2011

Ailis's Anterins i the Laun o Ferlies,
Alice in Synthetic Scots, tr. Andrew McCallum, 2013

Alice's Carrànts in Wunnerlan,
Alice in Ulster Scots, tr. Anne Morrison-Smyth, 2013

Alison's Jants in Ferlieland,
Alice in West-Central Scots, tr. James Andrew Begg, 2014

Alice muNyika yeMashiripiti,
Alice in Shona, tr. Shumirai Nyota & Tsitsi Nyoni, 2015

Алисаның қайғаллыг Черинде полган чоруқтары (Alisaniñ qayğalliğ Çerinde polğan çoruqtarı), *Alice* in Shor, tr. Liubov′ Arbaçakova, 2017

Alicia's Adventuras en Wonderlandia, *Alice* in Spanglish, tr. Ilan Stavans, 2021

Alis bu Cëlmo dac Cojube w dat Tantelat, *Alice* in Şurayt, tr. Jan Beṯ-Ṣawoce, 2015

Alisi Ndani ya Nchi ya Ajabu, *Alice* in Swahili, tr. Ida Hadjuvayanis, 2015

Alices Äventyr i Sagolandet, *Alice* in Swedish, tr. Emily Nonnen, 2010

'Alisi 'i he Fonua 'o e Fakaofo', *Alice* in Tongan, tr. Siutāula Cocker & Telesia Kalavite, 2014

De Aventure Alisu in Mirvizilànd, *Alice* in Uropi, tr. Bertrand Carette & Joël Landais, 2018

Ventürs jiela Lälid in Stunalän, *Alice* in Volapük, tr. Ralph Midgley, forthcoming

Lès-avirètes da Alice ô payis dès mèrvèyes, *Alice* in Walloon, tr. Jean-Luc Fauconnier, 2012

Lès paskéyes d'Alice è payis dès mèrvèyes, *Alice* in Central Walloon, tr. Bernard Louis, 2017

Anturiaethau Alys yng Ngwlad Hud, *Alice* in Welsh, tr. Selyf Roberts, 2010

I Avventur de Alìs ind el Paes di Meravili, *Alice* in Western Lombard, tr. GianPietro Gallinelli, 2015

U-Alisi Kwilizwe Lemimangaliso, *Alice* in Xhosa, tr. Mhlobo Jadezweni, forthcoming

Di Avantures fun Alis in Vunderland, *Alice* in Yiddish, tr. Joan Braman, 2015

Alises Avantures in Vunderland, *Alice* in Yiddish, tr. Adina Bar-El, 2018

אַליסעס אַוואַנטורעס אין וווּנדערלאַנד (Alises Avantures in Vunderland), *Alice* in Yiddish, tr. Adina Bar-El, 2018

Insumansumane Zika-Alice, *Alice* in Zimbabwean Ndebele, tr. Dion Nkomo, 2015

U-Alice Ezweni Lezimanga, *Alice* in Zulu, tr. Bhekinkosi Ntuli, 2014

www.ingramcontent.com/pod-product-compliance
Lightning Source LLC
Chambersburg PA
CBHW020336260626
47156CB00004B/1560